'Thank you

Piers stood for
her with that ra
won him man
began to stamp
hand and ruffled her hair. My p
Goodnight,' he said, and he walked away.

Christina climbed the stairs to her room, her face flushed. Oh, God! She had almost willed him to kiss her. How could she have been such an idiot?

Grace Read has had a lifelong love-affair with nursing. Starting as a Red Cross nurse in a London hospital during the war, she went on to do her general training in the Midlands. Marriage and a baby ended that career, but she retains a keen interest in the profession. Her youngest daughter is a nursing sister and keeps Grace abreast of modern trends, vetting her novels for medical accuracy.

Recent titles by the same author:

MAJOR INCIDENT
ONLY ONE CURE

CRISIS POINT

BY

GRACE READ

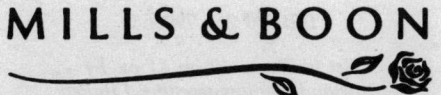

MILLS & BOON LIMITED
ETON HOUSE, 18-24 PARADISE ROAD
RICHMOND, SURREY TW9 1SR

DID YOU PURCHASE THIS BOOK WITHOUT A COVER?
If you did, you should be aware it is **stolen property** as it was reported *unsold and destroyed* by a retailer. Neither the Author nor the publisher has received any payment for this book.

All the characters in this book have no existence outside the imagination of the Author, and have no relation whatsoever to anyone bearing the same name or names. They are not even distantly inspired by any individual known or unknown to the Author, and all the incidents are pure invention.

All Rights Reserved. The text of this publication or any part thereof may not be reproduced or transmitted in any form or by any means, electronic or mechanical, including photocopying, recording, storage in an information retrieval system, or otherwise, without the written permission of the publisher.

This book is sold subject to the condition that it shall not, by way of trade or otherwise, be lent, resold, hired out or otherwise circulated without the prior consent of the publisher in any form of binding or cover other than that in which it is published and without a similar condition including this condition being imposed on the subsequent purchaser.

MILLS & BOON, the Rose Device and LOVE ON CALL are trademarks of the publisher.

First published in Great Britain 1995 by Mills & Boon Limited

© Grace Read 1995

Australian copyright 1995   Philippine copyright 1995
This edition 1995

ISBN 0 263 79036 3

Set in Times 10 on 11 pt. by Rowland Phototypesetting Limited Bury St Edmunds, Suffolk

03-9504-51078

Made and printed in Great Britain

CHAPTER ONE

THAT first week on duty at North Downs Hospital in Kent had been quite a challenge for Christina. She was glad it was behind her. Not since her first day at the primary school near Sydney, on the other side of the world, had she felt so lost. But that was eighteen years ago and now, amazingly, here she was back in England and working not far from the famous city of Canterbury where she had been born.

In her makeshift room at the nurses' hostel, standing in front of the square mirror on her dressing-table-cum-desk, Christina prepared for her last late shift before days off. She brushed her heavy flaxen hair into a ponytail, fastening it with an elasticated toggle, then reapplied a pink lipstick to her pleasantly curving mouth. Lastly she pinned her Australian College of Nursing badge to her Saxe blue uniform and stuffed a variety of working tools into the pockets.

Closing the door of her room on leaving, Christina found herself face to face with her neighbour across the corridor, a tall staff nurse she had seen about but not yet spoken to. They both smiled.

'Hi!' the girl said in a friendly manner. 'I'm Judy. You new here?'

'Yes—newish. I'm Christina Linden. I've been here just over a week.'

They fell into step, walking along and going downstairs together. The sun streamed across their path as they pushed through the outer doors and into a blossom-strewn, warm late May day.

'Gorgeous, isn't it?' Christina enthused. She breathed in the fragrant air, thinking yet again that the English countryside seemed to have put on a special show to welcome her.

'Yes, great. Too nice to be working.' Judy eyed the newcomer's honeyed complexion. 'You look as if you've been soaking up the sun somewhere,' she said. 'Have you been on holiday?'

Christina laughed. 'It began that way. I was staying with a friend who lives in London, near Hyde Park. But I guess I brought my tan with me. We do have bags of sunshine where I come from.'

She went on to explain about her recent arrival back in England. 'My friend Penny and I trained together in Sydney. Then she married a doctor who took a job over here. So Penny was able to give me a guided tour of all those places my mother used to tell me about, which was very convenient.'

Judy looked mildly surprised. 'What brought you here to work, then—wasn't there anything going near your friends?'

'Oh, I didn't try,' Christina said. 'I always intended to come over here. It's a kind of nostalgia for me. It's where we used to live before my folks emigrated. And my mother trained at North Downs, although it's grown a bit since those days,' she added with a smile.

'Where are you working?' Judy wanted to know.

'Men's Medical, although it seems more like Unisex to me. Mixed sexes on an open ward—my mum would have been horrified,' Christina said, laughing.

'Mmm—know what you mean,' the other girl agreed. 'Wouldn't care for it myself, but these days, with beds in short supply, you've got to get patients fitted in somewhere. I'm in Casualty so I see the other side of the story, trying to get people admitted.' She ran a despairing hand through her cropped dark hair. 'Hectic, but I wouldn't work anywhere else.'

They had by now skirted the large grassed area in front of the main hospital buildings where they paused on reaching the A and E Department.

'Well, this is where I love and leave you,' Judy breezed. 'Hope you're going to like it here. We must get together for a drink some time. See you around.'

'Sure. Bye for now.' Christina went on her way, happy at having made a new contact. At five minutes to one o'clock she was joining the oncoming staff to hear the hand-over report in the cluttered office off the entrance to Acute Medical. Thank goodness she was beginning to know her way around the sprawling environs of the hospital and its many departments. It was the jumbled geography of the place which was confusing, not the nursing itself. Health problems knew no boundaries and doctors and nurses talked much the same language wherever you were.

Sister Helen Yates, a large woman waging a constant battle trying to fit her generous figure into her navy blue uniform, bounded in and sat down at her desk with a stoical sigh. For the benefit of the assembled nurses she briskly reported on the progress of the patients in their care.

'And lastly we're expecting two admissions. Mr Ben Taylor is due to come up from A and E—he's query duodenal ulcer. Thelma Grant is being transferred to us from Intensive Care. She's an eighteen-year-old—was comatose for a week after an RTA but is making progress now. No room in Women's Medical, and that's positively our last bed unless we move someone out.'

The sister passed a hand over her round, amiable face and lifted back a straggle of brown fringe from her forehead. 'This is my half-day, if I ever get away. It's been like removals day in here all morning. We've spent our time rearranging beds.' Her brown eyes turned to the newest member of staff. 'Do you get this sort of upheaval in Australia?'

Christina laughed softly. 'Sometimes—but I've

never come across this kind of arrangement—I mean mixed sexes on an open ward. Where I was working it was broken up into two-, four- or six-bedded units, or single rooms.'

'Well, we're properly supposed to be all male here, but we have to co-operate if Women's is full, and vice versa.' The sister paused to take a phone call, then, 'Karen Hill reported sick this morning,' she went on, 'and they can only send me an auxiliary. That means you'll have to take over, Christina, when Patrick goes off at teatime. Still, you seem to have settled in OK and they're a good team on here. Any problems, just ask.'

Christina smiled in the direction of Staff Nurse Patrick Heywood, who gave the summer-skinned girl a friendly wink. 'You get off and enjoy your weekend, Helen,' he said. 'We'll survive.'

'At least, barring emergencies, you shouldn't be troubled with medics.' Helen paused. 'See if you can get someone to tidy up that television-room while visitors are here, Pat. It was an awful mess last time I looked in. And Christina, you had better primary nurse the new patient—Ben Taylor—when they bring him up. He's to go there.' She nodded towards a vacant place within easy reach of the nurses' station. 'Dr Conrad will probably be up to see him later.'

'Dr Conrad? Don't think I've met him yet,' Christina said.

'No? Oh, that's right, he's been away. He's our senior medical reg. Prof Burnley's firm. He's OK.'

The sister pushed back her chair and sped off to attend to some last-minute business before leaving. The remaining staff went about their routine tasks, checking vital signs, dispensing drugs and injections, wheeling non-ambulant patients to the bathroom, getting others back to bed and whipping away the odd left-over lunch dish before the arrival of visitors.

Christina's new patient, Mr Ben Taylor, arrived as visitors began to trickle in, and the casualty nurse accompanying him was Judy, her friendly neighbour from the nurses' hostel.

'Hi!' Judy said cheerily. 'This is Mr Taylor. His wife's with him. I asked her to wait in your TV-room until you've got him into bed.' In a quieter tone she went on, 'He's on Haemacell for now, but he's to go on whole blood a.s.a.p., I heard Conrad say. His haemoglobin's way down.'

'What's his blood type? Has it been ordered?' Christina queried.

'Yes, he's been cross-matched for four units. It's all in the notes.' Judy handed over the folder and departed.

When the porters had transferred the frail, ill-looking patient from the trolley to his waiting bed, Christina introduced herself as she plumped up the pillows behind him and arranged the covers.

'Hello, Mr Taylor,' she said in a welcoming fashion. 'I'm Christina. I'll be looking after you today. I just need to check a few details, then your wife can come in and stay with you until the doctor arrives.'

An anxious half-smile flitted across his lean cheeks. 'Never expected to find myself here, Nurse.'

'No, I don't suppose you did. I'll get a pillow to support that arm for you in a minute,' she said, pushing the drip-stand into a better position. 'Oh!' She paused, catching sight of a rangy, dark-haired man striding purposefully towards them. Despite his casual fawn cords and lack of a white coat, she guessed who he was by the stethoscope bunched in his jacket pocket. She was normally uninhibited by the medical fraternity, but something about this manly individual made her pulse quicken. She was about to greet him when he swished the green-striped curtain around his side of the bed and motioned Christina to do the same on hers, barely acknowledging her except as someone to take orders.

She felt affronted, while doing as he asked and putting more effort into the task than was strictly necessary. Appealing he might be; on the other hand there was a certain arrogance underlying the charm. However, the patient was ill and that was all that mattered. There was no place for pique in times of crisis.

'Good afternoon, Doctor,' she said civilly, 'Mr Taylor and I have hardly had time to say hello to each other as yet.'

Piers Conrad lifted dark, curving lashes to cast a level glance in her direction. 'No, I suppose not,' he returned, his hazel eyes making searching contact with the steady blue-grey gaze opposite, quite obviously sizing him up. 'May I have the notes, please?'

She passed over the folder, finding herself totally disarmed by that mildly seductive voice, so at odds with his masterful presence.

The registrar asked a few relevant questions of his patient while consulting the notes. Christina waited in silence for whatever was required of her, absently admiring the doctor's upright bearing and firm jawline.

'Right!' Piers Conrad said at length with a reassuring smile towards the patient. 'As you were told downstairs, Mr Taylor, your haemoglobin's in need of a quick boost. We'll get some blood into you and you'll soon be feeling a lot better.'

'Thank you. Am I—going to need an operation eventually?' the patient asked, his bottom lip trembling.

Piers Conrad patted the man's hand. 'Let's wait and see how you do on medication first,' he said kindly. 'We'll get you started on the blood for now.' Swishing back his side of the curtain, he addressed his remarks to Christina, handing her back the file. 'Send for it straight away, will you? And I'd like the first unit to run through in two hours. All right?'

'Yes,' she nodded, leafing through the notes to confirm the details.

Once more his arresting hazel eyes sought hers, lingering longer than he understood why on their luminous softness. 'Fine. I'll leave you to get on with it, then,' he murmured, and strode briskly away.

Christina returned her attention to the patient. 'I'll send your wife in now,' she told him pleasantly, and after directing Mrs Taylor to her husband's bedside she hastened to the office to find Patrick, the senior nurse. 'Dr Conrad wants this blood given stat,' she told him. 'How do I go about getting it?'

Patrick leaned back in his chair and stretched lazily. 'Send someone to the path lab for it. You'll need to fill in one of these first,' he added, leaning forward and singling out a request form from among the many in a paper-rack. 'I'll check the details with you.' He watched as she filled in the ward, patient's name and number, units required. 'That's right, kiddo. No porters about this afternoon. Send Rachel; I don't think she's too pushed.'

'OK, thanks.' Making for the ward in search of the third-year student, Christina cannoned into Dr Conrad in the corridor.

'Sent for that blood yet?' He raised a questioning dark eyebrow.

'I'm just going to find someone to send.' She waved the request form and wished she could have been on the way with it herself; but trained nurses didn't leave the ward to run errands.

Piers tutted. 'I'd hate to be in your hands in a matter of life or death,' he remarked drily. 'Come on, now. Chop, chop!' He was gone before she had time to see the twinkle in his eyes.

Pink-cheeked and heaping coals of fire on the heads of uppity doctors—one in particular—she sped on to find the student, who was in the sluice washing her hands. 'Rachel, please will you shoot to the path lab and collect this blood for me? It's for the new patient, Mr Taylor. Dr Conrad wants it started now if not yesterday.'

Rachel giggled and dried her hands carefully before dropping the paper towel in the bin. 'What's new?' she said. 'Must go to the loo first.' Stripping off her plastic apron, she tucked the form into her uniform pocket and ambled off towards the staff toilet.

Sighing, Christina could only hope that the registrar wouldn't show up again until the blood had arrived and they had got the transfusion nicely flowing.

Meanwhile, the expected eighteen-year-old patient from ITU had been transferred and was waiting by the office in a wheelchair, escorted by parents and possessions and a large vase of flowers.

Patrick approached Christina. 'Angel, I'd earmarked this lass for Rachel, but would you mind doing the honours until she gets back? Her name's Thelma Grant. She's to go in that far corner bed, next to Mrs Janes—it'll be company for them both. Thanks, pal.' He gave her an ingratiating smile as she obligingly went to see the new patient into bed.

'Hello, it's Thelma, isn't it?' Christina smiled at the parents and stooped to greet the wan-faced teenager. It brought no expression to the girl's blank brown eyes. She sat twisting a strand of her long brown hair which was held back with a dark blue bandeau. There was fading bruising around one of her eyes but otherwise her face was unmarked. 'We've got a bed for you next to a very nice lady,' Christina went on. 'I'll show you where it is.'

'You won't get anything out of her, Nurse,' her anxious mother volunteered as they wheeled the girl to her appointed place. 'She's not talking yet, but she's marvellous to what she was, isn't she, Jim?'

Her husband nodded. 'I don't like her being put in a men's ward, though. Not very nice for a young girl, is it?' he said disapprovingly.

Christina shrugged. 'It's the problem of finding a bed. But we'll take special care of her, don't you worry. It might even arouse her interest, seeing a few guys around. Does she have a boyfriend?'

'Yes—he was driving the car when they had the accident,' the father growled. 'He's in the orthopaedic ward with a broken leg and crushed ribs.'

'Oh, dear!' Christina shook her head sympathetically.

Having settled the girl into an armchair beside the bed, she was relieved to see Rachel back from her errand and coming to take over.

'Did you get it?' she asked.

'Yes, two units. I put it in the fridge.'

'Great—thanks.' Christina introduced the student and explained that Rachel would be looking after Thelma for the time being, after which, leaving Rachel to complete the necessary paperwork, Christina was able to go ahead with changing Mr Taylor's transfusion.

Double-checking with Patrick that they had been supplied with the correct blood group for the right patient, she wheeled her prepared trolley to the bedside.

'That's all right, Mrs Taylor,' she said when the patient's wife asked if she should leave. 'This won't take me long. I just have to change the tubing.'

Expertly she made the change-over, renewing the giving set to the appliance tapped into a vein at the back of Mr Taylor's wrist, replacing the Haemacell transfusion with a unit of the cross-matched whole blood.

Watching with interest while Christina flicked the new tubing to rid it of any air bubbles before connecting it, Mrs Taylor asked, 'Do you think I could have a word with his doctor, Nurse? I didn't get a chance downstairs.'

'Yes, I'm sure you can, if he's still about. When I've finished here I'll see if I can find him.'

Satisfied that the drip was running smoothly, she adjusted the flow to the required number of drops per minute, rebandaged the cannula site and made the patient's forearm comfortable on a pillow. 'Right—now I'll leave you in peace,' she said with a warm smile, and wheeled her used trolley away.

An orderly was about to start on her round with the tea and coffee dispenser as Christina made for the sluice-room. 'Queenie, have you seen Dr Conrad in your travels?' she asked the jolly West Indian.

'Yes, love. In his office with the girlfriend,' Queenie laughed. 'I just took 'em in some tea.'

'OK, thanks.' Hastily Christina deposited her equipment, washed her hands and went to catch the doctors before they could disappear. She knocked on the door and looked in, finding Piers Conrad in discussion with Amy Gillow, his house officer, a diminutive, attractive girl even with a voluminous white coat over her neat figure.

They both glanced up. Piers said, 'Yes, Nurse?'

'Sorry to butt in, but Mrs Taylor would like to speak to you about her husband, when you're free.'

He nodded. 'Tell her I'll be along presently.'

Christina flashed him a smile of thanks. Well, at least he was approachable, even if his sense of humour was open to question. Far too good-looking for his own or anyone's good, of course. And she found herself wondering what his relationship with Amy was. Queenie's tag of 'girlfriend' had been just a figure of speech. All the same, they were two attractive people. . .

Going for her own tea-break before Patrick went off duty, Christina tried, yet again, to telephone the home of her aunt Beth, her mother's sister who lived at Herne Bay. She had tried on a number of times, unsuccessfully. This time, however, she was in luck, a male voice answering.

'Hello! Is Mrs Beth Wells there, please?' she enquired brightly.

'Sorry—no,' was the answer. 'Can I take a message?'

'Yes, if you wouldn't mind. Will you tell her that her niece Christina called?'

There was a pause from the other end before a surprised voice queried, 'You mean—Christina from *Sydney*?'

She laughed softly. 'Yes, that's me.'

'Well, hi there!' the speaker returned, sounding delighted. 'This is Justin. Where are you speaking from?'

'The North Downs Hospital—I'm working here.'

'Good heavens! I didn't even know you were in England. Nobody tells me anything.'

She laughed again, rather liking the sound of her cousin Justin. 'Actually, your mother doesn't know I'm here either. I thought I'd surprise everyone. Get myself established in a job over here first, so that I didn't have to be an embarrassment if—er—things didn't work out. You know what I mean—my mother and yours were not exactly bosom pals. Sibling rivalry, probably. But before she died Mum said she wished they could have been closer.'

'Mmm,' Justin murmured. 'We were all really shocked to hear about her—being taken ill so suddenly like that. We were wondering only the other day how you'd been getting on since. Look, we must get together. It's just luck I happened to be here when you rang. My folks are away on holiday at the moment and I'm keeping an eye on the place, as promised. But I've my own flat in Canterbury, which is where I work. When are you free?' he asked. 'Can we meet?'

'Yes, I'd like that. I'm off tomorrow and Monday. Any use?'

'Fine! How about lunch tomorrow?' her cousin enthused. 'Better come and pick you up, hadn't I?'

Christina smiled into the telephone, feeling a glow of excitement. 'Yes, that would be lovely.'

They agreed the time and place and postponed further chat until their meeting. Thrilled at last to have begun what she had set out to do, Christina hurried to the canteen to have her tea before returning to work.

Patrick handed her the ward keys. 'There you are, pal, all yours. Everything's OK. Should be all peaceful once the visitors go.'

She slipped the keys into her uniform pocket. 'Thanks, Patrick. I'll be fine. Don't worry.'

The senior nurse grinned. 'Never do, once I leave this place. Have fun.'

The rest of the day passed smoothly enough. Short-staffed though they were, the remaining nurses worked conscientiously, needing no prompting to get on with their work. With the visitors gone by eight o'clock Queenie began taking around the bedtime drinks while the nurses straightened beds, shook up pillows and updated charts.

Going to check on Mr Taylor's pulse-rate, Christina saw that his blood pack would need renewing shortly. The reserve in the fridge was the one now in use. Thinking she ought to send for a further supply, she was wondering who could be spared when Rachel came to find her.

'Chris—would you come and have a look at Thelma?' the third-year said, looking troubled. 'I've just got her back into bed and changed her nightie for her. I checked her pulse and it seems very sluggish. In fact she seems a bit odd—I mean more so than before.'

Oh, no! Please don't let her collapse on us. Christina sent up the fervent prayer as she stepped smartly towards where Rachel had drawn the curtains around the young patient's bed. With head injuries anything was possible.

'All right, Thelma?' she began, parting the curtains.

The teenager lay back against her pillows, knees hunched, eyes open but vacant, her face pallid. Even as Christina spoke, the girl slipped sideways into a crumpled heap.

In a flash Christina was by the bedside, catching the helpless girl under the armpits. 'Quickly, Rachel—get those pillows away!' she rapped out, sounding a great deal calmer than she felt. 'Let's lie her flat.'

'What is it—a faint?' Rachel queried, hurriedly throwing out the bedding and pushing back the bed-rest.

Christina didn't answer, concentrating on the grey-faced patient, turning her head to one side. Years of training prompting her actions, Christina checked the radial pulse. She found it with difficulty and her own heart hammered painfully when it suddenly came to her that Thelma had stopped breathing.

A respiratory arrest! Schooling herself to remain cool, she issued instructions in a quiet, controlled voice. 'Rachel, get me the ward resus trolley—and get someone else to phone for the crash team. Hurry.'

Rachel fled away as though demons were at her back. Meanwhile there was no time for Christina to waste time waiting for help. If an impending cardiac arrest was to be prevented, it called for mouth-to-mouth, or those four precious minutes to avert brain damage would be lost.

Without hesitation she began the vital first-aid measure, hyper-extending the girl's chin, closing the nostrils and breathing steadily and rhythmically into Thelma's mouth. Patiently she continued with her efforts until her breathless assistant returned with the required equipment.

'Queenie's phoning the crash team,' Rachel panted.

'Right. Pass me the Brook Airway and that Ambu-bag—then raise the foot of the bed. . .'

After carefully inserting the airway into the teenager's throat, Christina positioned the manual resuscitator and began to squeeze the bag. Relief flooded over her as colour began slowly to return to the ashen young face of their patient.

Hurrying footsteps signified the arrival of the crash team in a bold dash to the casualty, but by this time immediate danger had passed and what might have been a calamity had been held at bay. Even so it was a tremendous relief to hear Piers Conrad's authoritative voice asking questions, and to hand over responsibility to him and the duty anaesthetist. All Christina had now to do was relate the events which had led up to the emergency and follow instructions.

When all that needed to be done was done and Thelma was once more breathing normally it was decided, as a precautionary measure, that she should go back to ITU for the time being.

'Although the nurses here seem to have been on their toes. Well done, girls,' approved Dr Will Mason, throwing a pleased smile in their direction as he departed.

With the crisis over and the patient returned to Intensive Care, it was back to their interrupted ward work for the nurses.

'Phew!' Rachel breathed, wiping sweaty palms on the skirt of her uniform. 'Don't know how you managed to stay cool, Christina. Did she really actually stop breathing?'

'Maybe for just a minute.' Christina's skin prickled again at the memory. One never got used to the urgent demands for action in a crisis. There was always that racing of the pulse, that feeling of inadequacy. Now she felt like a limp rag, drained of strength. 'Smart of you to call me when you did, Rachel. You'll make a good nurse,' she said, giving praise where it was due.

The student flushed with pleasure. 'Oh, well, back to bedpans and bottles,' she laughed.

The night staff had by now arrived and Christina went to the office to give the hand-over report and write up her account of the happenings. It wasn't until the other day nurses had left the ward that she remembered Mr Taylor's blood had yet to be collected from the path lab.

'I would have sent for it but for that emergency,' she told the night staff nurse.

The other girl groaned. 'That's all I need, with only one auxiliary. I'll have to see what the NO can organise. . .'

'Don't worry. I'll get it for you myself,' Christina said.

'Would you? I'd be awfully grateful.'

'Sure, no problem.'

They exchanged smiles and Christina felt she had made an ally. One couldn't have too many of those when you were a stranger in a strange land.

Later, her errand accomplished, Christina collected her belongings from her locker and went off duty content at having left nothing undone. She also realised how hungry she was, but after the trauma of the last few hours eating out on her own in the local Pilgrim's Rest was the last thing she felt like doing. No, it would have to be a snack and a coffee in her room, then bed.

Her thoughts were interrupted by that same disturbingly assertive voice which had issued emergency instructions to her about an hour previously.

'So, maybe you won't be such a dead loss to us after all!' Piers Conrad jokingly remarked, coming up behind her as she was about to leave the building.

She turned to look at him as the automatic doors slid back. 'Gee, thanks. If that was meant to be a compliment,' she added with a wry grin.

They paused together on the forecourt outside. He eyed her askance, one dark eyebrow lifting. 'Late going home, aren't you?'

'I went to the path lab for some more of Mr Taylor's blood, for the night staff.'

'Oh!' He paused. 'They breed dedicated nurses in Oz, do they? And which part of the Antipodes spawned you?'

'Not any part of it,' she countered, smiling. 'As it happens I was born under a gooseberry bush not too many miles from here.'

The registrar clicked his fingers in feigned annoyance. 'Wrong again, Piers. But that's not where you've been hanging out for the past few years, I'll bet.'

'No—it was Sydney as a matter of fact. Why? Are you an expert on linguistics?'

'Not at all, but the inflexion isn't hard to pick up.' His forthright hazel eyes had a roguish gleam. 'Anyway, welcome to the team,' he said.

'Thank you. Goodnight.' She turned and walked off in the direction of the nurses' hostel.

Piers Conrad's eyes followed her. In the silvery light of an almost full moon her blonde and bouncy ponytail was fascinating. He would have liked to pull off that restraining band and see the bright locks fall about her pretty face. But that was a road down which he had no wish to tread again. Resolutely he made for the car park, *en route* to his bachelor flat.

Christina, after her light exchange with the registrar, was quite encouraged. She thought things might be shaping nicely workwise after all. Tomorrow, though, and the meeting with her cousin Justin, that was another matter. He had sounded great over the telephone, so there was no reason for this vague feeling of apprehension which she had. A feeling that she might just be about to open Pandora's box!

CHAPTER TWO

IN A coral-pink summery dress, her fair hair loose about her shoulders, Christina waited for her cousin that Sunday lunchtime, outside the nurses' hostel, as arranged. Being early, she stood gazing in the direction of the car park, her feelings a mixture of curiosity and apprehension. She could dimly recall that studio portrait his mother had sent—Justin in academic dress when he had graduated—but what kind of person he would turn out to be she had absolutely no idea.

A few minutes later she had no difficulty in recognising the tallish, lean young man who strolled towards her. Aged twenty-six, her cousin was two years older than Christina—and not short of cash, was her first impression, judging by his appearance. Stylish leisure trousers and a fawn leather jacket sat easily on his loose-limbed frame and his straight brown hair was expertly cut.

He approached her with an engaging grin. 'Excuse me. . .Christina?'

She smiled happily in return. 'Yes—and you must be Justin. Hello!' Feeling oddly shy, she didn't know quite how to greet him, so held out a welcoming hand.

Justin set the tone of things immediately by leaning towards her and kissing her lightly on the lips. 'Hi! Great to see you.' Laughingly he slid an arm around her waist. 'I was just trying to remember the last time we were together. I think it was my eighth birthday party. . .'

'When you pushed me into the fishpond and ruined my party dress,' Christina finished for him, her grey-blue eyes merry. 'You were a little horror in those days.'

He chuckled. 'I'm much nicer to little girls these days, I promise you.'

Conversation flowed readily between them, there were so many years to catch up on.

Leading the way to where his red open sports car was parked, he asked, 'How long have you been in England?'

'It's well over a month now. I was in London for a few weeks, staying with my friend Penny. We trained together in Sydney,' Christina chatted, 'but she married an Australian surgeon who's working over here for the moment.'

Justin manoeuvred his car through the maze of vehicles and out of the hospital grounds. 'Why didn't you let us know you were planning a visit? I would have been there to meet you.'

'We-ell. . .' Christina hesitated. 'I thought it might be better this way. Penny was able to show me the sights, the touristy things and the West End shops, before I got down to the serious business. Actually,' she went on, 'I wanted to get established in my job and somewhere to live here before getting in touch with you all. Didn't want to be a nuisance to anyone.'

'You wouldn't have been that, I'm quite sure.' Justin flashed her a beguiling smile, which had Christina sensing that her cousin liked the ladies.

They were now nearing the historic city nestling behind the remains of its ancient ramparts, the towers of the great cathedral dominating the landscape. Justin found a space in one of the perimeter car parks and they began walking towards the hotel where he'd reserved a table.

'Mind how you go in those shoes,' he advised, eyeing the slender heels on Christina's summer sandals. 'Some of the streets around here are what you might call rustic.'

It was Christina's first visit inside the walled city. She stepped warily along narrow pavements, the flagged stones worn silk-smooth by centuries of feet. More often than not there was no room to walk in anything but single file. Fascinated, she gazed about at the criss-crossing alleyways and lanes crammed with a myriad small shops, and at the gabled houses with blackened beams which leaned at crazy angles towards the roadway.

Reaching the square with the romantic name of Buttermarket, Christina paused, awestruck by the splendour of the medieval gateway to the cathedral grounds. 'Wow! Look at that!' she exclaimed. 'I've seen views of various places on calendars and in books, but the real thing—that's *unreal*!'

Her cousin laughed and hustled her along. 'Come on. You'll have to join one of the guided tours if you're interested in history. Right now we've got a date with some lunch, and a lot of our own history to catch up on.'

Arriving at the prestigious hotel of his choice, they left behind the relics of the past for the comforts of the present. Over their meal in the elegant gold and white dining-room Justin plied her with questions as to what had prompted her to come to England.

'It's a case of back to my beginnings, I suppose.' Christina finished her excellent fresh salmon salad and drank some wine while thinking of the best way to explain. 'I do have a lot of good friends in Sydney, but now that my mother's gone I had no sense of belonging there.'

Justin rested his elbow on the table and propped his chin on his fist, looking thoughtful. 'What about your dad? I know their marriage broke up soon after you all went to Australia, but didn't he keep in touch with you?'

'I know he meant to—but he died in a boating accident about a year after leaving.' Christina frowned. 'I'm sure my mother must have written...'

Her cousin looked suitably mortified. 'Oh, yes, *sorry*. I've a hazy recollection, but it probably happened while I was away at school. One loses out on the family info with not being around at the time.' He paused reflectively, waiting until the waiter had gathered up their plates and moved away. 'So I see that does leave you on your own. Must be over a year now since your mother died...'

To her embarrassment Christina felt tears threatening as she remembered that time. Her mother's worsening headaches, and the horrendous day when an inoperable brain tumour had been diagnosed. Within two months her beloved mother had gone to her Maker. Even though they had led separate lives since Christina started nursing, the house near to the country hospital where her mother had been matron had always been home to Christina—the place where she was sure of a loving welcome. Oh, help! I mustn't cry, she told herself. Biting her bottom lip, she managed to regain control

Justin reached over to touch her hand. 'Sorry! It must have been awful for you—especially having to cope on your own.'

She managed a limp smile. 'It's OK. I had lots of support from our friends. Thought I'd got over being emotional. It's probably being here, among the places she used to talk about, making me sentimental.'

The waiter brought the sweet trolley, which created a diversion and lessened the tension for both of them.

'One of the last things Mum told me before—er—the end was how much she regretted not being able to come back and see her own parents before they died,' Christina went on presently. 'She'd been promising herself to come and see Aunt Beth before this illness came out of the blue. That's mainly the reason I decided to come. I felt she would have liked me to, although I know they had their differences.' She gave Justin an enquiring glance. 'I never managed to find out exactly why that was. Do you know?'

Her cousin's answering smile was evasive. 'No, I just picked up the odd innuendo now and then. Not worth repeating. All water under the bridge now, anyway.' Diplomatically he veered away from the subject. 'My mother's asthmatic—lives on pills. Surprises, even nice ones, are apt to put her in a flap, so perhaps it was a good thing that you got me when you rang that day,' he pronounced blithely. 'When they get back from holiday I'll explain things to her. Get her used to the idea of seeing you before she hears from you.'

'Yes, I did know about the asthma.'

Christina's back was to most of the other tables in the busy dining-room, whereas Justin had a clear view of the other diners. His glance strayed over her shoulder. 'Don't look now,' he said in a teasing manner, 'but there's a guy over there who keeps looking in this direction. Not anyone *I* know. Must be fascinated by *you* is all I can think. Not that I blame him. You're very easy on the eye, dear cousin.'

She giggled. 'And you've got a smooth line in chat, *dear cousin*. Let me know when it's all clear to look.'

He shook his head emphatically. 'No, no, *no*! Much too obvious. Patience, please.' Justin's eyes sparkled mischievously. 'He's with quite a dishy bird—and her mummy and daddy by the look of it. Family celebration perhaps? Can't have you mucking it up.'

'O-oh!' Christina rolled her eyes and laughed. 'I'd forgotten how exasperating you can be.'

They finished their dessert and were directed through to the lounge for coffee. Rising, Christina turned casually—and her eyes met those of Piers Conrad seated at his table for four.

Giving a slight smile, the registrar inclined his head in acknowledgement. She smiled in return, and felt a degree of satisfaction at having her personable cousin by her side as they left the dining-room.

'Oh! So you *do* know that guy?' Justin murmured in her ear.

'Yes and no. He's the registrar on the ward where I'm working. We met for the first time yesterday, so I can hardly say I know him. But we have met.'

'And once seen never forgotten.'

Christina smiled and paused to smell a spray of white lilac in the massive pedestal arrangement of hothouse flowers which decorated the attractive lounge. 'Perhaps he was wondering if it *was* me. On duty I tie my hair back. Can't have it loose like now.'

They chose a low sofa for two, near to the flowers, and a waiter arrived promptly with their tray of coffee.

'What about the girl—do you know her too?' Justin asked idly.

Christina poured their coffee. 'No, can't say I noticed her particularly, except that she had long curly brown hair.'

'Mmm. Great, wasn't it?' her cousin mused.

'What made your parents move to Herne Bay?' Christina wanted to know.

'Dad was made redundant when the advertising firm he worked for was bought out. He'd always fancied living on the coast. Mum wouldn't go too far away or she said they'd never see me, so Herne Bay it was. He's set up his own photographic studio there. You missed them by a week, as a matter of fact. They've gone to Florida—be back in a fortnight.'

Piers Conrad and his party had also come through for their coffee, taking seats further on into the long room.

Justin's eyes followed the girl while Christina made

a determined effort to concentrate her attention on her cousin. 'And what kind of work do you do?'

'Not a lot, if I can help it,' he joked. 'No, seriously, I'm with a building society. Suits me fine. I like contact with people and one gets to meet all kinds. If you're wanting a flat, Christina, just let me know.' He flicked in annoyance at something which buzzed noisily around his head. 'What's that?'

'Looks like a bee, I think. Must be your aftershave that appeals to him.'

'More likely those flowers,' he said, continuing to wave his hand around. 'Where did it go?'

She saw that the insect had actually come to rest on Justin's shoulder. She was wondering how best to get rid of it when he caught the direction of her gaze and brushed quickly at his jacket. The bee reacted fiercely. In the next instant Justin clapped a hand to the side of his neck. 'Ouch! Bloody hell! The wretch stung me.'

'Oh, dear! Let me see.' Jumping up, Christina went to investigate. The bee had flown off, but left its sting behind. It was protruding from the flesh just above her cousin's collar. 'No, don't rub it, Justin,' she warned, pushing his hand away. 'The sting's still there. I'll have it out in a jiff.' Hastily she searched in her cosmetic purse until she found her tweezers.

Her cousin was making a pained face. 'God! It feels like somebody jabbed me with a bunch of red-hot needles. . .'

'Well, hold still a minute.' Carefully she applied her tweezers and lifted out the sting with the remains of the tiny poison sac attached. 'There! Now what you need is a nice cold pad soaked in sodium bicarb—that would ease the pain,' Christina sympathised. 'They may have some in the kitchens here. I'll get the waiter to ask. . .'

'Oh, let's not make a fuss.' Justin found a handkerchief and mopped his brow. 'Finish your coffee and we can get out in the fresh air. Warm in here, isn't it?' He ran a finger around the inside of his collar and loosened the top button. 'Sorry about this, but I'm beginning to feel sort of—well, rotten, really. You wouldn't have any paracetamol in your bag of tricks, I suppose?'

Christina began to feel uneasy. Beads of sweat were beginning to form on his upper lip and there was an air of desperation about him. 'Sorry, no,' she said, 'but there may be a dispenser in the cloakroom. I'll go and. . .'

'It's OK. I'll go myself. . .' Justin got to his feet. 'Could do with a cold rinse or something.'

He walked a little unsteadily towards the door. There he paused, holding on to the door-frame; then his knees seemed to sag and he slid down into a distraught heap on the rich gold carpet.

Unaware that their little drama had been attracting attention, Christina found herself forestalled by Piers Conrad when she rushed to help her cousin.

'What exactly happened to him?' the registrar asked, on his knees beside the writhing Justin, who was gasping for breath.

'Stung by a bee, on the neck,' she returned, her eyes wide with alarm. 'Must be allergic. Do you have any adrenalin with you?'

He reached for the bunch of keys in his pocket and waved them at the girl who was about to follow him over. 'My emergency bag, Donna. In the boot of my car, please.'

While the girl sped away Christina helped the doctor to lay her cousin in the recovery position. Justin's face was pale and clammy and he was making weak, incoherent sounds, trying to clutch at his throat.

Piers exchanged glances with Christina. 'Phone for an ambulance,' he ordered quietly.

She needed no urging. Racing to the reception-desk

telephone, she made contact with the emergency service, stressing the gravity of the situation.

Meanwhile, in her absence the girl called Donna had just arrived back, breathless, with the registrar's medical case. Quickly Piers sought out and administered the crucial injection. There was no immediate, miraculous response. Justin now lay inert.

'Did you know he was allergic to insect stings?' Piers gave Christina a look of enquiry.

She shook her head despairingly, smoothing back the moist brown hair from her cousin's puffy face. 'I know his mother's asthmatic, but Justin isn't. Oh, heavens! What an awful thing to happen. Where's that wretched ambulance?' she appealed wildly.

Piers checked his wristwatch. 'It is only five minutes since you called them,' he pointed out, maintaining professional calm while inwardly being as impatient as she was. 'I'll give him another injection if it's not here soon.' Timing Justin's pulse, he found it fast and thready, but made no comment.

Presently, at the welcome, unmistakable wail of the approaching ambulance siren, they all sighed with relief.

'Won't be long now,' Piers said thankfully. 'He'll be getting oxygen soon. I'll give him some more adrenalin—and they'll put him on antihistamine IV once he gets to Casualty.'

His companion, Donna, hovered uncertainly, her round young face full of concern. 'Oh, I *do* hope he's going to be OK,' she fretted. 'One feels so totally useless, not being able to do anything.'

'You were quick about getting my case. That could prove extremely useful.' Piers rewarded her with a somewhat preoccupied smile.

It crossed Christina's mind to wonder where his car was parked for the girl to have been so quick. Justin had left his car some distance away.

Within minutes the ambulance crew were being directed to them by the fluttering restaurant staff. After advising the paramedics of the precise dosage of the drugs he had given, the registrar handed Justin over to their care.

'And you're going with him, are you?' Piers studied Christina's troubled face with kindly concern.

She nodded. 'Yes. Thanks for your help.' And she followed the stretcher-bearers out to the waiting ambulance.

Later that day, her cousin now happily recovering, Christina sat beside him in the day ward attached to A and E. There was an oxygen mask in position over his face and he was receiving the vital intravenous antihistamine injections. Once at the hospital no time had been lost in dealing with Justin's allergic emergency, but Christina was well aware that had not Piers Conrad happened to be on hand at the outset things might have been very different.

Judy, her new friend from the nurses' hostel, had been assigned to monitor Justin's progress. Coming to check his blood-pressure, and hearing about the registrar's timely help, she remarked, 'That was a turn-up, wasn't it? I mean, a doctor being on the spot when needed! Your boyfriend's guardian angel must've been really on the ball,' she laughed.

'Actually, Justin's not my boyfriend, he's my cousin. And goodness knows how I'd have faced my aunt if we hadn't managed to get him here in time.' She felt almost light-headed with relief now that the immediate danger was over.

Justin, who had been lying peacefully with his eyes closed, now opened them. Pulling forward his oxygen mask, he murmured, 'How long will they be keeping me here?'

'Probably just overnight, all being well,' Judy

surmised. 'You may have to come back for some anti-venom vaccine, as you seem to be susceptible.'

'Oh! The thing is—about my car, Christina. That was a long-stay park I left it in—but I don't want to get clamped.' He paused for breath. 'It's a firm's car—insured for any named driver. Do you drive?'

'Yes—you'd like me to collect it and park it somewhere else for you?'

'Please. If you brought it back here, then I could drive it home when I leave. The keys are in my back trouser pocket.'

'OK. I'd better do that now, then, hadn't I?' She reached into the locker cupboard, found his folded trousers and the keys in the hip pocket. 'Tell me the name of the place where we left it.'

'Dover Street. If you take a taxi they'll know where that is.'

'Will do!' Christina returned brightly. She patted his hand. 'Be good till I get back.'

Walking through the casualty waiting area on her way to the telephone, she found the imposing figure of Dr Conrad coming towards her. 'How's your friend?' he asked.

The concern in his steady hazel eyes made her want to hug him. She breathed an exaggerated sigh of relief. 'Recovering, thank goodness!'

He smiled. 'Ah! I thought you looked moderately more cheerful.'

'Thanks again for what you did,' she began in a flurry of gratitude. 'Heaven knows what would have happened if you hadn't been there. Sorry if it messed up your lunch party.'

'We were more or less at the end of it in any case,' he returned dismissively. 'And now where are you dashing off to? Anything more I can do?'

Christina pushed both hands through her tumbled fair hair. She was beginning to flag after the strain of events. She was beyond wanting to make polite small talk, and she had a job to do. 'No, thanks,' she said with a tired smile. 'I'm on my way back to Canterbury to collect Justin's car.'

'Oh! How are you getting there?'

'Just going to phone for a cab.'

'Well, if you'll wait half a minute I'll run you in there myself. I'm going back in any case. My father is staying at the hotel and he left his camera in my car. I'll just check on your friend before I go. Won't be long.'

While he was gone she used the time to tidy her hair and cool down a bit. Admittedly, she would rather have gone by taxi than be beholden to him yet again, but he had left her no choice. In any case, since he had said he had to go back, it was a sensible suggestion, wasn't it?

'That young man had a narrow squeak,' the registrar chatted when they were on their way back to the city. 'Anaphylactic shock is relatively uncommon after stings. We must fix him up with an aerosol inhaler for use in an emergency.' He gave Christina a brief sideways smile. 'That was your *second* life-and-death scenario in as many days, wasn't it?'

She frowned, casting her mind back. 'Oh, you mean Thelma's respiratory arrest. Is she OK now?'

'I hope so. Apparently it was a reaction to one of the drugs she'd been on.' After a pause, Piers asked idly, 'Is that guy very important to you?'

'Justin?' Christina smiled to herself. 'Very—although not in the way that perhaps you were meaning. He's my cousin.'

'Oh! So you do still have family connections over here?'

'Yes. An aunt and uncle and Justin.'

His lips puckered humorously. 'I get your drift. I imagine you wouldn't have been too popular with the parents had the worst happened.'

Christina grinned back. 'You certainly know how to boost a girl's confidence.'

He laughed. 'You're not lacking in that, I'm quite sure. Although I must admit you look more vulnerable with your hair down.'

Her colour deepened and she was glad that he needed to keep his eyes on the road. To change the subject she asked, 'Were you celebrating something at lunchtime? You all looked very festive.'

'Yes, it was their first anniversary—my father and his new wife, that is. Donna is my stepsister. You'll probably see her around the hospital from time to time. She's a student nurse,' Piers explained. 'She's doing her practical assignments at North Downs.'

'Oh! Nice for her to have you on her doorstep. It helps to have a friendly expert handy.'

'Is that experience speaking?' he asked lightly.

'Well, yes, in a way. My mother was a nurse. Actually she trained over here, before we went to Australia. She ended up being matron of a community hospital in NSW,' Christina added.

'So what decided you to come back here?'

Damn! She didn't want to go into all that. He was probably only making polite conversation. Nevertheless, there seemed no way to avoid answering. Various plausible reasons suggested themselves before, finally, she decided on a plain statement of fact as the easiest option.

'My mother died about eighteen months ago,' she told him. 'I wanted to visit her only sister—Justin's mum. It was meant to be a nice surprise, but they're away on holiday at the moment. So you can see that if Justin had popped off while in my company...' Christina patted her heart and shuddered theatrically. 'How could I ever have faced them?'

Piers was silent for a while, taking in this information. 'Mmm, that would have been gruesome for you. But your cousin survived,' he added cheerfully, 'so you can stop worrying.'

They were nearing the ancient city walls once more and soon their brief intimacy would be over. Christina was thankful for that, although in a strange way she had found him easy to talk to. He was an attentive listener. He was also extremely charismatic and his quirky smile seemed calculated to set her nerve-endings tingling. She hoped he wasn't also a thought-reader!

The registrar pulled to a stop a short way from the entrance to the car park she directed him to. 'You'll know where to find your cousin's car among this lot?'

She nodded. 'Not difficult to recognise. It's a bright red sports job—and I've got the reg number.'

His neat dark brows narrowed. 'Have you driven on these roads before?'

'No, but we drive on the left in Australia, so I shouldn't have any problems.'

'Would you like me to wait here and lead you back?' he offered.

'Thanks, but I'll be fine, really.' Christina let herself out of the car. She wasn't exactly as confident as she sounded, but she was damned if she'd let him know it.

'You follow the Old Dover Road, that way,' he pointed as she sketched him a light wave of farewell. 'It's a one-way system out of here, remember.'

She had to admit to being glad of his last-minute directions as, after taking time to familiarise herself with the workings of the strange car, she manoeuvred her way out of the city and drove back towards the hospital. It was, in fact, enjoyable to be behind the wheel again after having had to depend on public transport and other people since she'd been in England. It was time to get wheels of her own again as soon as possible, she decided.

Justin's car was at last safely delivered to the car park adjacent to the nurses' hostel. Feeling weary, Christina slipped back to her room to freshen up before going over to the day ward to return the car keys and check on her cousin's progress. The duty sister was glad to report that he was continuing to improve, but they were carrying on with the antihistamine treatment as a precautionary measure.

With the foot of his hospital bed still raised, Justin lay with his eyes closed until Christina touched his hand and softly spoke his name.

'Hello!' he said with an embarrassed half-smile. 'Excuse my not getting up. They say I must keep lying down, although I'm feeling OK now.'

'Well, three cheers for that!' Christina beamed at him. 'I've collected your car, Justin. And I didn't scratch the paint. There you are.' She laid the keys on the bedside cabinet. 'It's where you left it when you came to pick me up this morning. All ready for when you're able to drive away.'

'Thanks. You're a pal. Sorry to be giving you all this dashing about. And you still manage to look a million dollars,' he said admiringly. 'Not like me in this gear.' Her cousin fingered his examination gown with distaste.

She laughed. 'Sure sign you're better if you care what you look like. Anything else I can do for you?'

'Er—I was wondering,' he began, 'what happened about the bill for our lunch? Did you pay it?'

She clapped a hand to her mouth. 'Oh, help! No, I didn't. With all the commotion of getting you here in a hurry, the bill was the last thing on my mind.'

'And the last thing *I* remember was feeling bloody awful, and your doctor and his girlfriend staring at me...'

Christina laughed. 'You may be interested to know

that she's not his girlfriend. She's his stepsister. Her name is Donna.'

As she was telling him this, she caught sight of the girl herself hesitating in the doorway. Christina smiled in her direction and the younger girl came eagerly to join them.

'Excuse my butting in,' she said, lifting back her wealth of brown hair and looking directly at Christina. 'Sister said it would be all right, but do say if I'm a nuisance. Only, with my being there when it was panic stations, sort of thing, I wondered how your friend was getting on.' She turned a charming smile on Justin. 'Looks better than he did, doesn't he?'

'Certainly does,' Christina agreed laughingly. 'All he's worried about now is that our lunch bill didn't get paid.'

'Well, he can stop worrying about that,' Donna said in her best patient-soothing voice. 'It's taken care of. Dr Conrad paid it.'

'He did?' Justin, who had been gazing at the girl spellbound, recovered his powers of speech. 'That was jolly nice of him. If you'll find out for me what the damage was, I'll let him have a cheque.'

The two beamed at each other. Christina felt superfluous.

'Expect I'll be leaving here in the morning,' Justin said suddenly. 'You'll need to know how to get in touch with me. Christina, would you mind? In my jacket pocket there should be some business cards.'

Christina felt for and found the required card. Justin wrote his home telephone number on the back. 'There you are, Miss. . .?'

'My name's Donna,' she said. 'Donna Bryce.'

'Justin Wells. Christina and I are cousins,' he hastened to explain.

'I know. Piers told me. Well. . .' She smiled at him sweetly. 'I'm just so glad you're OK.' She put her hands together in supplication. 'Wasn't it fantastic that my stepbrother happened to be on the spot at the right time?'

'Wonderful,' he agreed, not able to take his eyes off her, 'and thank you for coming. You will let me know, won't you, about the bill?'

She said that of course she would, and after a further exchange of pleasantries Donna left them.

Watching her go, Justin gave a satisfied sigh. 'What a stunner! And to think if that little brown bee hadn't zonked me we might never have met. Funny how life works out, isn't it?'

Christina couldn't help laughing. 'I hope it works out to your satisfaction, Justin. As of now, all Donna has agreed to do is tell you how much you owe Dr Conrad for our lunch.'

'Everything has to have a beginning.' Justin smiled languidly. 'You didn't mind, did you? I mean about me asking her to sort it out.'

'On the contrary, I was rather glad you did. After all, Dr Conrad is the senior medical registrar here, and I'm a new girl. He's already gone out of his way to help me today. I'd prefer to keep a low profile for a bit. Don't want anyone to think I'm being pushy.'

Justin turned on his side to get a better look at her. 'I bet he enjoyed playing Sir Galahad. You mustn't underrate yourself, little cousin.'

She gave a soft laugh. 'He just got lumbered because he was there—but thanks for the boost to my morale.' She watched as he stifled a yawn. 'It's been quite a day, hasn't it?'

'Yeah, it sure has.'

Christina rose to go. 'I'll push off, then, and let you get some rest. I'm free tomorrow. I'll enquire in the morning about when they're letting you leave, in case there's anything you need. In any case, I'll look in to see you some time. Sweet dreams.'

'Thanks. Don't I get a goodnight kiss?'

Smiling, she brushed a token kiss on his cheek. 'I wonder who you take after—your mum or your dad?'

'Oh, definitely my dad,' Justin said. 'He's always had an eye for a pretty face.'

Waving a cheerful goodbye, Christina left him. But her jaunty step was out of keeping with the sudden, strange sense of foreboding that crept up on her. It was that last rejoinder of her cousin's which struck a chord of distant memory. She recalled something her mother had said, after receiving a letter from her sister, about Aunt Beth having had a lot to put up with, and Uncle Henry being a lovable rogue.

Christina wondered if the same remark might apply to Justin. Unwittingly, it was she who had been responsible for Donna's meeting him. She hoped nobody lived to regret it.

Piers also came into her mind. Would he approve of those two getting together—if they did? True, Donna was his stepsister, but they weren't blood relations, should he fancy her himself.

But she was being ridiculous, wasn't she, letting her imagination run away with her? And in any case the people concerned were consenting adults. It had nothing to do with her.

CHAPTER THREE

COMPARED with Christina's eventful days off, returning to the routines of ward life was like coming back to sanity. Here at least stressful problems were not her own, although they might often be a strain on the emotions. But that was entirely different from being personally involved.

Apart from a lively telephone chat with Justin, who had called her after he was back at his flat, she had heard nothing from him since, so presumably all was well with him. He had promised to let her know as soon as his parents were home. It was now just a question of waiting.

Later that week Christina and Patrick were in the office with Sister Yates, discussing admissions, when they were interrupted by an internal telephone call. After a fairly lengthy dialogue Helen sighed as she put down the receiver.

'That was A and E,' she told them. 'They'll be sending us a CVA—Mr Chalice, aged fifty-four—on Dr Conrad's say-so.' She considered for a moment, chewing the end of her ballpoint. 'We'll have to move Mr Taylor down the ward, I think. We can probably leave it until he goes for his gastroscopy, but tell him what to expect, will you, Christina?' The sister glanced sideways at Patrick. 'We're also to get an overdose when they've finished washing her out. Girl of nineteen. That'll rock the boat again for Piers, eh?'

Patrick smiled wryly. 'Maybe! Let's hope this one's not one of the broken hearts brigade.'

Christina looked from one to the other but said nothing although she couldn't help feeling curious. She assumed there must have been an attempted suicide which had disturbed the registrar more than usual.

Explanations might have been forthcoming but for the arrival of elderly consultant Professor William Burnley on one of his infrequent ward rounds. With him were Piers and Amy Gillow, Piers' house officer, and the consultant's secretary—a primly suited auburn-haired woman with notebook at the ready.

'I'll take the notes trolley,' Patrick murmured to Christina as the sister went out to meet the group. 'No need for you to hang about—unless you'd like to, that is?'

'No, thanks,' Christina returned quickly, 'I've got plenty to do—and I'm not totally genned up on everything as yet.'

When the doctors and nurses had moved off down the ward Christina went to tell Mr Taylor about his forthcoming bed move.

'You'll be in a different place in the ward when you come back from your gastroscopy, Mr Taylor. It's a sign you're getting better, the further up you go,' she told him cheerfully. 'We'll make sure your locker goes with you, and all your bits and pieces, so don't worry.'

He caught her hand as she was about to move on. 'This—whatever it is I'm going to have, Nurse—that young woman doctor was babbling on about it to me yesterday, only I didn't have my hearing aid in at the time. She seemed a bit rushed, so I didn't like to bother her with questions. What does it entail exactly?' Mr Taylor's lean cheeks creased with anxiety. 'Will I be conscious? Will it be painful?'

'The gastroscopy?' With a confident smile Christina sat down beside the bed. 'No, Mr Taylor, it won't be painful, and it's nothing to be alarmed about. You'll be given an injection which will make you sleepy before they start. All that happens is the doctor will pass a thin, flexible tube through your mouth, down your throat and into your tummy. There's a light on the end of the tube so that he can see what's going on down there and what caused your bleeding. You won't feel a thing, and when you wake up you'll be back here with us. All right?'

'Oh! And supposing—I mean, whatever they find, they wouldn't decide to operate while they've got me on the table, would they?'

Christina laughed softly. 'Good gracious, no! You'd need a lot more preparation for major surgery. They'll probably take a tiny bit of tissue for analysis, though. What we call a biopsy. That's all.'

The patient relaxed visibly. 'Oh, yes, I know about those. My wife had one for her breast lump, and that turned out to be benign.' His smile broadened with relief. 'Thanks, love.'

'Anything else you want to know, don't be afraid to ask.' She stood up to leave him. 'I'll be getting you into an examination gown once we know what time they want you. And robbing you of your teeth then, of course.'

'Do you mind?' he exclaimed with mock-indignation, 'They're all my own.'

They were both in giggles over her mistake when the consultant and his entourage arrived at the foot of Mr Taylor's bed.

Professor Burnley regarded them beneficently over the rim of his half-moon spectacles. 'That's what we like to see,' he approved. 'Patients with smiles on their faces. Good afternoon, sir. May we share the joke?' The professor's bedside manner was as polished as his sleek silver hair. His pale blue eyes twinkled enquiringly in Christina's direction.

Christina knew it wouldn't be protocol to engage him in small talk. 'Just a private *faux pas*, sir,' she murmured, controlling her grin.

'I see. We all make those from time to time, don't

we?' The professor turned to his registrar. 'What is the situation here?' he asked.

Piers Conrad, whose attention at that moment was focused on Christina, promptly brought himself back to ward business. His deep voice modulated to a confidential level, he began his assessment of the patient's symptoms, and while the doctors conferred Christina seized her opportunity to slip away.

She had not been unaware of the registrar's attention; their eyes had met briefly as she'd left the bedside. Now, deep in thought about the charismatic Piers, she ran into Rachel coming from the linen cupboard, clean sheets in her arms.

'Oh, Christina, would you have a minute to help me get Thelma up?' Rachel appealed. 'Her bed needs changing.'

'Of course.' Thelma had been transferred back to them from Intensive Care the previous day. 'How does she seem?' Christina asked as they walked together down the ward to where the young hemiplegic patient lay, her face as expressionless as ever.

The student nurse shrugged. 'She seems to hear, and I think she understands, but she doesn't respond. Sad, isn't it? I wondered if it would help if we could push her to see her boyfriend?'

'Might be a bit soon for that,' Christina murmured. 'Besides, I don't think her parents were too keen on the guy, from what I heard her father say. We don't want to stir up trouble.'

Keeping up a cheerful conversation, they drew the rainbow-striped curtains around Thelma's bed and helped her into dressing-gown and slippers. Her left arm and leg were heavy and useless. Placing a blanket over her knees, they propped the useless arm on a pillow on her lap.

During their attentions Thelma's heavy dark hair had become disarranged and Christina sought out the girl's brush and comb. 'Must make you smart for your visitors,' she said, brushing back the tousled locks, being careful to avoid the colourful bruising on the right of her forehead. 'There, that's beaut,' she declared, finishing off with a fresh bright hairband.

Rachel had found a perfume atomiser in Thelma's toilet bag. 'Le Jardin,' she read. 'Mmm—that's nice.' And she sprayed some behind the girl's ears.

But for all the nurses' fussing around her there was no reaction from their patient, just the same blank expression. They drew back the curtains.

Mrs Janes in the next bed was liberal with admiration. 'My word, you look really smashing, Thelma. The girls have done you proud.' Confidentially, she wheezed, 'I keep trying to get her to talk, you know, but she won't.'

'Early days, Mrs Janes, but we'll get there.' Christina gave the woman a warm smile before hurrying away to answer the ringing telephone and reassure an enquiring relative.

The doctors had by now left the ward. The large hot-trolley with patients' lunches had arrived and meals were served in accordance with diets. Helen then sent Patrick to first lunch while she herself sped off to a sisters' meeting.

'I shouldn't be too long,' she told Christina, 'but if that CVA should arrive before I get back you'll have to get on with moving Mr Taylor.'

The expected stroke victim, Mr Chalice, was actually brought up within ten minutes of the sister's departure, which had Christina and one of the auxiliaries flying around to make the necessary changes. But at last all was in order and a comforting cup of tea supplied to the patient's anxious wife.

With admission charts and identity bands still to be made out, Christina returned to the office to complete the paperwork. Absorbed in her task, she was unaware that Piers Conrad had come back until his rugged frame blocked out the sunlight shafting through the doorway. As she looked up, pen poised in her hand, a surprised smile curved her lips.

'Hello!' she exclaimed, feeling an irrational glow of pleasure at his presence. 'What can I do for you?'

He strolled in and parked himself on one of the metal-framed chairs, letting his hands rest lightly between his knees. 'I see Mr Chalice is here.'

'Yes—his wife's with him.' She half rose. 'Do you want to look at him now?'

He waved her down. 'Presently.' His long-lashed eyes met hers. 'How's your cousin?' he enquired.

'Fine, as far as I know. We haven't been in touch for a day or two.' All sorts of questions flashed through her mind, but the uppermost one was about their lunch bill on the previous Sunday. 'Thanks for your help the other weekend,' she said. 'I was told you also paid for our lunch. Donna promised to take it up with you and let Justin know what he owed. Has he done that yet?'

Piers leaned back, hands behind his dark head. 'Yes—that's been settled.' His shapely mouth twitched ironically. 'Cupid has strange ways of shooting his dart.'

She felt a little uncertain. 'You mean—the way Justin and Donna seem to have hit it off? I—I've no idea if it's gone any further. Hope you won't mind if it does. I don't know too much about him,' she added. 'That was the first time we'd met for eighteen years.'

The registrar shook his head. 'It's nothing to do with me whom she dates, although I've known her since she was a kid. Our families were neighbours. My father and her mum joined forces after their respective partners died.' He pulled a wry face. '*If* I were asked for my opinion—which I haven't been—I think Donna would be wiser to concentrate on her RGN before getting dewy-eyed over a new boyfriend.'

'Oh!' Christina smiled at his guarded criticism. 'Does she have lots?'

'I believe there's a plentiful supply of escorts. Perhaps there's safety in numbers.' Piers gave a self-conscious grin. 'Do I sound like a spoil-sport?'

She laughed softly. 'I can understand your feeling a certain responsibility. I should think Justin's harmless—if any guy is, come to that,' she added.

'Spoken with hindsight?' His dark eyebrows lifted in enquiry.

'No—just observation.'

'Yes, a disreputable bunch, aren't we?' He suddenly switched to more immediate matters. 'This young overdose girl we're expecting—where are you putting her?'

'Sister said in one of the side-wards—unless there's anyone for discharge today.'

Piers stroked his chin thoughtfully. 'A side-ward would probably be best, until she gets herself sorted.'

Christina's grey-blue eyes were touched with compassion. 'What did she take, and why?'

'Paracetamol. Quite a fistful. I gather it was a *cri de coeur*. No man is worth that kind of sacrifice.' He rose to go, his expression inscrutable. 'Be nice to her?'

'Naturally.' Christina felt her cheeks grow warm under his level gaze. 'It's not our business to moralise. Everyone makes errors of judgement at some time or other.'

Piers made no reply, but his eyes meeting hers seemed to be searching out her hidden thoughts. At that moment uppermost in her mind was Helen's remark that this patient might stir up memories for the registrar. She suddenly felt the need to drop her gaze and sort through the papers on the desk.

'You'll do!' he remarked crisply.

Helen, returning from her meeting, broke up the difficult moment, freeing Christina to take her own lunch-break. For a moment there she'd had a sense of walking on eggshells. She wished she knew why.

Down in the crowded canteen Judy waved to her from the table she was sharing with Yvonne, another nurse from Casualty. 'Room over here!' she called.

Glad to be invited, Christina carried her light meal over to join them. Talk around the table was light-hearted, concerning the forthcoming centenary fair which was organised annually for the hospital by the Society of Friends. This year the effort was to be extra-special, it being the centenary year.

'They want us to get up teams for a sort of *It's a Knock-out* competition. There's a notice on the staff-board,' Judy said. 'The winning team will get a special donation to spend on whatever they'd like for their ward.'

'How much is that likely to be?' Christina asked.

'Depends on what's required, I suppose. Why, have you got any bright ideas for your ward?'

'Well, I'd like to see the layout rearranged—beds properly curtained off into decent-sized bays, so that we could give the patients more privacy.' Christina bit into her toasted cheese sandwich. 'The last thing I would want if I were sick would be some strange guy gaping at me from across the aisle.'

'Mmm. Must be a bit off-putting,' Yvonne agreed. 'In the new wing most of the wards are divided up into four- and six-bedded bays. In your case, though, it would probably mean closing the ward while they did it. With the present bed shortage I can't see the management agreeing to that.'

'Surely they have to close wards sometimes, for the essential spring-clean, don't they?' Christina said.

'Suppose so. Anyway, expect you'll have a meeting about it. Put your idea forward.' Yvonne jumped up from the table. 'Coffee everyone? I'll get it.'

'How's that cousin of yours?' Judy asked when the other girl had left them. 'A real charmer, isn't he?'

Christina laughed. 'Oh, not you too. He seems to have made a hit with Dr Conrad's stepsister as well.'

'Who's that?'

'Donna Bryce—one of the second-years. She came in to see him while he was in the day ward—remember?'

Judy's eyes widened. 'She's Conrad's stepsister? Well, what do you know? We had her working in A and E some time ago. Nobody mentioned she was related to him, though.'

'Perhaps they prefer it that way,' Christina said.

Yvonne returning with their coffees, the conversation reverted to the centenary celebrations and the Grand Ball which was to follow. But time had slipped away and their lunch-break was almost over. With still much to talk about, Judy suggested they should meet again that evening at the Pilgrim's Rest, the sixteenth-century inn which was a regular haunt of the hospital staff. That agreed, they parted company in good spirits.

As she arrived back at work, Christina's cheerful mood was promptly dispelled by the sound of strident voices coming from the television-room. Startled, she paused by the open doorway *en route* to the main ward. The only occupants were two men, both in their mid-forties and obviously in heated argument. The more solidly built of the two had a menacing attitude as he jabbed a finger towards the other, a well-groomed man in an expensive grey suit.

'Why don't you bloody well clear off?' he barked. 'You've done enough damage as it is. I warned Sophie not to trust you. She was an idiot ever to fall for your claptrap.'

'Now look here, Mr Branch, I've said I'm sorry.' The grey-suited arms were held wide on a shrug. 'What more can I say? I'd been trying to cool things between us for some time—to let her down lightly, you know. Although she threatened suicide if we broke up I never thought she'd go through with it.'

The father's voice rose to a bellow. 'She's just a kid, for God's sake! Nineteen last birthday. You took advantage. Y-you, and your money, and your lies. You ought to be horse-whipped! And if anything happens to her I swear I-I'll——'

Christina thought it high time to intervene.

'Excuse me,' she began politely, taking a step into the room, 'would you please mind lowering your voices? Who is it you've come to see?'

'My daughter Sophie, Nurse.' There was a catch in the father's voice. 'Sh-she's taken pills—tried to do away with herself on account of this—this *scum*!' His eyes glittered with hatred as he glared at the man facing him. 'I'm damned if I'm going to let him see her. *I'm* her next of kin. I've every right to stop him, haven't I?'

The offender adopted a conciliatory attitude. 'Mr Branch, I'm as heartsick about this as you are. Surely you won't begrudge me the chance to make amends—to do what I can for Sophie, in the circumstances?'

'You stay away from her. Do you hear me?' Although more controlled, there was a threat in the father's manner. He raised a clenched fist, his jaw jutting.

Alarm prickled Christina's skin. Stepping further into the room, she said reasonably, 'It's quite possible your daughter may not be well enough to receive visitors just yet.' She laid a hand on the father's arm. 'If you'd like to come with me, sir, I'll see if I can find out what the position is.' Turning to the other man, she went on firmly, 'And if you wouldn't mind waiting here, Mr——?'

'Stoner,' he returned. 'Tell her it's Matthew, and I'm here if she would like to see me.'

Christina took the irate parent along to the interview-room. 'I know this must be very distressing for you,' she said gently. 'Would you mind waiting here while I make enquiries?'

Closing the door quietly, she went in search of Sister Yates. Afternoon visitors were beginning to trickle in as she checked the office and found only Patrick there. In answer to her query as to Helen's whereabouts, he jerked a thumb towards the side-ward.

'In there, with Piers and the OD girl. What was all that commotion just now?'

'The girl's father and her boyfriend having an argument.' As she spoke Dr Conrad and the sister both came from the side-ward.

'Christina!' Helen exclaimed. 'I was just coming to find you. This new admission—Sophie Branch—she's fully conscious now. Will you clerk her in and look after her? She's not likely to be co-operative, but do your best.'

'Yes, Sister.' Christina looked from Helen to the straight-faced Piers, slipping his stethoscope back into his pocket. 'I've just separated her father and a Mr Stoner. They were getting heated—thought it best to part them before they came to blows,' she said. 'Her father's in the interview-room and would like to see someone. The other man is in the TV-room.'

The registrar scratched his cheek resignedly. 'I'll see the father, Helen. You can deal with the other one.' He switched his gaze to Christina. 'In the interview-room, did you say?'

She nodded. 'He's very angry.'

'You could hardly blame him for feeling murderous,' Piers snapped back.

Sister Yates gazed after him as he left, her mouth twisting ruefully. Sighing, she turned her attention to Christina, reeling off details of the new patient's condition.

'It seems she took around thirty paracetamol, and some Co-proxamol, washed down with red plonk. The boyfriend went round to her flat when she didn't show up for work today—she was his secretary. He said he'd spoken to her at seven o'clock this morning so hopefully she wasn't too far gone to prevent liver damage. She's on Parvolex IVI, and Naloxone. Fifteen-minute baseline obs for the time being, Christina, and Piers must be called if her systolic pressure falls below eighty.' Helen handed over the notes. 'Now I suppose I must go and talk to this chap who brought her in. He's probably feeling terrible.'

The sister went off towards the TV-room, leaving Christina to make herself known to the patient.

On entering the side-ward Christina saw a small, desolate figure in an examination gown; she was huddled against a flat pillow, her straight fair hair in disarray. The cot-sides of the bed were up, the foot raised, and a drip-stand supported the intravenous line channelling life-saving drugs into the girl's forearm.

At that precise moment the patient was making a feeble, confused effort to dislodge the cannula securely splinted in place. Her blotched cheeks were puffy and wet with tears.

'Hello, Sophie!' Christina stepped swiftly to the bedside. 'Is that coming adrift?' she asked, lowering the bed-rail. 'Here, let me see. . .' And she replaced the ravelled piece of Micropore with a fresh strip. 'I'm Christina,' she said pleasantly. 'I'll be looking after you for now.' She took the girl's hand in hers. 'Are you beginning to feel a bit better?'

Sophie snatched her hand away and burst into convulsive sobbing. 'Oh, g-get lost!' she choked. 'Let me die, for God's sake. Why won't they just let me die?'

Christina's own eyes grew moist. Swallowing against the lump in her throat, she stroked the girl's hair and spoke soothingly. 'I know, Sophie, you must have been feeling at rock-bottom. Want to tell me about it?'

Angrily, Sophie turned her face away. 'Get lost!'

she flared. 'I'm not talking to anyone. Stop pestering me! Go to hell!'

'Oh, come on, love,' Christina coaxed. 'I'm on your side. I'd like to help.' She paused before going on, 'You know, there are people feeling absolutely shattered to think you were driven to this. Your dad especially. He's outside. Wouldn't you like to see him?'

Sophie said nothing, biting her lip and sniffing in abject misery.

'There's also someone named Matthew,' Christina ventured. 'He said to tell you he was here. I believe he was the guy who found you and brought you in.'

That information at least caused a reaction. 'So it was him, was it? The sod. Why did he bother?' the girl whimpered. 'I—I hoped he'd be having me on his conscience for the rest of his life.'

'He probably will, even now,' Christina returned, offering a handful of tissues. 'You gave him an awful shock, whatever he did to deserve it.'

Sophie mopped her tears and blew her nose. 'H-he said he wasn't going to leave his wife after all,' she faltered. 'A-and he didn't want her finding out about us—said it would upset his precious family. I left a letter so everyone would know. But if he found me, I expect he found that. . .'

'He may have done. I don't know. But sometimes things happen for the best, Sophie. Now, love, I have to check your blood-pressure, et cetera, or I shall be getting the boot. Just let me wrap this sleeve around your arm. . .'

Chatting quietly, Christina made the necessary observations, and in between further bouts of tears Sophie's story unfolded. It was the usual tale—a married man of some affluence, promises made, and in the end the realisation that her lover had no intention of ever leaving his wife.

'I guess I've been an idiot,' the girl said, 'but I

couldn't help it. I really loved him. And he said he loved me.' She wept again.

'I'm sure he did,' Christina comforted. 'It's not impossible to love more than one person. Maybe it was easier to let go of you than his wife and family, but it must have been a difficult choice.' She paused. 'At least he's given you the chance to start again. Why not see your dad now? He badly needs to be comforted. I dare say he feels sort of guilty himself. Parents often do, when their kids are in trouble.' She handed the girl more tissues and shook up her pillow.

Sophie nodded. 'OK. He's brought me up since I was ten. I'm all he's got really.'

Some moments later Christina left father and daughter together while she wrote up her Kardex on the present state of the new patient.

'That Mr Stoner went home,' Helen told her. 'I said it would be best if he rang to enquire, but that Sophie wouldn't be here for more than a few days, all being well. Piers is arranging for psychiatric counselling once she's stabilised.' The sister ran her hands through her hair. 'Heigh-ho! What a day.'

That evening it made a pleasant break for Christina to meet Judy and Yvonne for a bite at the Pilgrim's Rest. The cosy saloon had a welcoming atmosphere, its plastered walls lined with photographs of past Kentish cricketers and polished horse brasses, the rafters garlanded with hop vines.

As usual, the place was busy. With Christina's circle of friends gradually widening, she felt relaxed and comfortable among this easygoing assembly of mainly off-duty hospital staff. In between talking to her companions as she ate her home-made quiche and salad, her gaze wandered in search of other familiar faces. But the face she was looking for—although not even to herself would she have admitted it—was not there.

Perhaps Piers Conrad didn't frequent this particular watering-hole. His friend Dr Will Mason obviously did, however.

In a chunky, colourful sweater and elderly jeans, Will Mason might have passed for any local talking cricket at the bar with the landlord, but Christina recognised him as the anaesthetist who had been with Piers on the crash team the day when she had needed to call them for Thelma, their collapsed head-injury patient.

He caught her eye as she glanced his way. They exchanged smiles, and Will sauntered over to their table, tumbler in hand. 'Hi, fellow workers! Shove up, Judy. Let me park my bones alongside yours for half a mo.'

Judy obligingly edged along the wooden bench to make room for him. 'Do you know Christina?' she asked.

'Hello, Christina!' Dr Mason's small brown eyes twinkled. 'So you're the one from down under?'

She smiled. 'Word gets around.'

'What do you think of us so far?'

'First impressions—OK.' Christina warmed to this laid-back character.

Will finished his drink and wiped his tidy moustache on the back of his hand. 'Your arrest the other day— she rallied magically after we changed the medication.'

'Yes, great. We've got her back again now. Not that her parents are too keen on her being put among the guys.'

The anaesthetist made a resigned gesture. 'Not much we can do about that, other than sending people miles away to another hospital. Some of the medics have been agitating for better ward layouts. You girls ought to do your own bit of agitating.'

'And be branded trouble-makers? You must be joking!' Judy hooted.

Will laughed aloud. 'Defeatist! Stand up and be counted.' He glanced at his wristwatch. 'Piers said he'd be coming over. Must've got held up—or perhaps he's gone into his shell on account of that latest OD we channelled through.'

Christina looked puzzled. 'Can somebody please tell me what it is about an OD that gets to Dr Conrad? Helen Yates hinted at something. . .'

The others looked at her askance. Then Judy exclaimed, 'Oh! Of course, you wouldn't know. It was before your time. About eighteen months ago, I think.'

Will took up the story. 'One of the secretaries developed an obsession with Piers. They'd had a good, friendly working relationship. He took her out a few times, but as far as he was concerned nothing jelled, and that was it. However, she read it wrong and started to become a nuisance. He thought it only fair to put her straight, and she went to pieces. When she threatened suicide Piers banked on it being emotional blackmail, but she overdosed—and nobody found her until it was too late.'

'Oh!' Christina was shocked into silence for a moment, then, 'How awful,' she murmured. 'That must have really slayed him.'

'Yeah, it was a pretty horrible experience,' Will said, 'and he didn't deserve it. He ended up vowing he'd never even date anyone else, in case they got the wrong idea.' The bleeper in his trouser pocket sounded urgently. 'Ah, well, duty calls. Must love 'n leave you, my children. Bye-bye!' He ruffled Judy's dark hair as he departed.

She smoothed her hair with an impatient hand. 'Why do blokes always do that?'

Christina smiled absently. 'Nice guy, though.'

Judy grinned. 'I saw him first, remember!'

'You're welcome,' Christina said, laughing. 'I'm not husband-hunting. I enjoy being a free agent.' But her thoughts were not concerned with Will, they were far away with the troubled Piers. She could imagine how devastated he must have felt, being the unwitting cause of someone's death. What a dreadful situation to have to live with.

CHAPTER FOUR

CHRISTINA ran her finger down the timetable located at the side of the bus shelter and saw that she had twenty minutes to wait for the next bus. Oh, well, it was only six-thirty and there were still a few hours of daylight left on this pleasantly warm June evening. Plenty of time for her to find her way around and see what there was to see. The journey to the village that had once been home shouldn't take long, once she had found the right connection at Canterbury.

Sitting on the slatted wooden bench, she crossed her jeans-clad legs and prepared to wait. The country highway not far from the hospital cut through pleasantly green meadows dotted with plump sheep and lambs, and the hawthorn hedgerows were white with scented blossom. It was a far cry from the lush, exotic landscape of the country she had left behind, where hibiscus flowers grew to the size of tea-plates and gaudy parakeets were so tame they would eat from your hand in the garden. But this place, despite the roar of traffic from the nearby motorway, had a serene beauty of its own. Something which had instantly appealed to her.

So too had North Downs Hospital, or rather the staff there. She had been made to feel very much at home. Despite the hectic pace of the past two weeks Christina felt that she could happily settle here, all else being equal. Yesterday Justin had phoned her to say that his parents were expected home any time now and that he'd let her know as soon as a visit would be possible.

Now, with a free evening and none of her new friends around, she thought she would try to find the house where she'd been born. Daydreaming, she didn't notice the white BMW until it pulled up with a screech of brakes some ten yards beyond the bus shelter, then smartly reversed to a halt in front of her. Piers Conrad leaned across to look out of the window.

'Where are you off to—like a lift?' he asked.

She jumped up with a happy smile. 'Oh, yes, please. That would be great—if you're going my way.'

'Depends which way that is,' he returned, a laugh in his voice. 'I'm on the way to Herne Bay.'

'Oh, are you? That'd do fine—if you don't mind me coming along,' she said, changing her mind on the spur of the moment.

'Not at all. Glad of the company. Is this one of your tours of discovery?'

'Mmm—I started out intending to find our old house at Blean, if it's still there. But I'd just as soon have a look at Herne Bay; that's where my aunt and uncle live. And you know what they say about never going back to a place. If I did it might ruin that perfect mental image I'd built up over the years.'

Piers chuckled—a deep-throated, infectious sound that had her laughing too. 'Well, it is a woman's prerogative to change her mind, I suppose.'

He was in a much better mood this evening than he had been when the young overdose patient was in his care. Sophie Branch had stayed with them for a couple of days. After some psychiatric counselling she had gone home yesterday with her father. All the time she had been there Piers had been short-tempered, barking at everyone. He'd even had Amy Gillow, his hard-working house officer, biting back the tears on one occasion. Even so, apparently everyone forgave him, making allowances because of that trauma in his past.

Glancing at him sideways, admiring his strong jawline, the alluring mouth now tilted in amusement, Christina tried to imagine how it would feel to know you had been responsible for someone else's death. Even innocently. Could you ever absolve yourself from the burden of guilt?

'So what are you going to do with yourself once you get to Herne Bay?' Piers went on amicably. 'Call in on Justin's parents?'

'Oh, no. They're not back from holiday yet. I'll just mooch around.' She paused. 'And you—is this business or pleasure—or shouldn't I ask?' He was dressed in a neat grey suit and white shirt, as befitted his professional status, not the casual clothes of someone bound for an off-duty date.

'Me? No, I'm not out to play. Prof Burnley landed me with one of his duty visits—a lady with a thyroid problem. She's at the local cottage hospital, but they'd like her transferred to North Downs.' The registrar was silent for a moment. 'It shouldn't take too long. If you'd like to come there with me, what would you say to a little mooch together, and then something to eat?'

After all she'd heard about his avoidance of dates since that unfortunate episode in his life, the suggestion took her by surprise. But then, he wouldn't class this as a date, would he? It was more in the nature of two people at a loose end—some company for them both. In his present frame of mind, however, she found him undeniably fascinating. Even the nearness of his physical presence in the confined space of the car made her sensually aware. Christina made a mental note to be on her guard against letting the feeling grow.

'That sounds great,' she said, smiling up at him. 'At least that way I shan't be in danger of getting stranded. I've no idea what the bus service is like here.'

'Neither have I. I've not much experience of the buses. You'll have to get yourself some timetables.'

'Get myself some wheels would be a better idea,' Christina said.

The BMW was spinning along smoothly, eating up the miles. They had actually bypassed Blean, the place she had originally set out to find, and were now on the fringes of Herne Bay, the small coastal holiday town.

'Well, that didn't take too long, did it?' Piers remarked conversationally. 'Do you know, I've been at North Downs for over two years and I've never had occasion to come this way before? Thank you, Prof Burnley, for broadening my horizons.' He paused for a moment, controlling a grin. 'Perhaps that should be thank you, Christina. I should probably have gone straight home again after this visit, if I hadn't seen you waiting forlornly by the bus-stop. You looked miles away,' he continued, giving her a sideways glance. 'Were you wishing you were back down under?'

'Far from it. I was just soaking up the scenery here and thinking about——' She broke off suddenly and changed the subject. 'Anyway, why isn't Professor Burnley doing his own visiting?'

'He's off on a lecture tour, to the USA. But I don't mind doing his donkey work. It keeps me out of mischief.'

With a determined effort Christina dragged her eyes away from the registrar's seductive good looks. She gazed out of the window to where birds were busy searching out grubs among the waving wild flowers on the grassy banks. There were tall white daisies and some dainty blue weeds which she didn't recognise.

'Those blue flowers—they're pretty!' she exclaimed. 'Do you know what they're called?'

He looked briefly. 'Sorry. Buttercups and dandelions are about the extent of my knowledge, botanically speaking,' he joked.

She tutted. 'Everyone should know something about their native flora. I'll have to buy myself a book. I just missed the best of the bluebells, so I was told,' she chatted on. 'My mother always raved about the bluebells.'

'Yes, they are quite spectacular in the spring. You'll have to stick around until next year if you want to see them.'

Piers had eased the car through a busy little high street with a wealth of fascinating small shops, the pavements still thronging with people on this bright Sunday evening. Ascending a long hill, they then turned off at a signpost pointing to the cottage hospital. Soon they were pulling up outside what could have passed for a country mansion but for directional notices in cream letters on brown boards. The surrounding gardens were neatly laid out and planted with floribunda roses in many different colours.

Piers parked in a space reserved for doctors. 'I shouldn't be too long,' he said, and, indicating his stock of cassettes, 'If you'd like some music, help yourself.' He then strode off towards the main entrance of the building.

Watching his loose-limbed, easy gait, Christina could scarcely believe that here she was, socialising with the charismatic registrar. Common sense told her that he must find her company agreeable or he wouldn't have suggested that they should spend the rest of the evening together. But even if he had forsworn romance there was no reason why he shouldn't have women friends, was there? In any case, tonight would probably be just a one-off, she decided.

Idly browsing through his collection of cassettes, she found Elton John, Nigel Kennedy and music from *Miss Saigon*, among others. Nothing much to be learned from that, except that his musical tastes were not too high-flown. She slotted in the *Miss Saigon* cassette, sat back and tried to concentrate on the music. All too often, though, her thoughts wandered, brooding about the strange ways of fate which had thrown her into close contact with the intriguing registrar.

It was some thirty minutes before Piers returned. 'Hello. You found something to amuse yourself, then?' He slid in beside her and she switched off the recording so that they could talk.

'Yes, I saw that show when I was in London. Loved it. Well, how was the patient?'

He stroked his chin, looking thoughtful. 'She certainly needs help. Seems like she's heading for thyrotoxicosis, poor lass. Woman of thirty, and just married. All the usual symptoms—highly nervous, rapid pulse, husky voice, protruding eyes, difficulty in swallowing. I've arranged to have her transferred to us. We'll need to put her through the specific thyroid tests, get her basal metabolism controlled, and then refer her for a partial thyroidectomy, I expect.' With a conscious effort Piers shelved the medical problem and started up the car. 'Right. Let's give this place the once-over, shall we? I hear the promenade recently had a face-lift.'

'This is my first visit to the coast since I've been in England,' Christina confided with eager anticipation. 'I'm looking forward to a glimpse of the sea again.'

Piers smiled indulgently. 'It's not one of our major resorts, I must warn you. Hope it doesn't turn out to be a big let-down. As far as I'm concerned this is much more agreeable than spending the evening sorting out case histories—which is what I ought to be doing.'

'Glad to be of service!' she returned playfully. 'Any time!'

'I'll bear that in mind,' he said.

It wasn't long before they were driving along a coastal road leading to the newly laid out esplanade. Here were artistically planned flowerbeds already bursting with summer colour behind neat little protective railings. People sat enjoying the evening sunshine and children were making good use of the activity toys in their amusement playground.

Christina's eyes roved in all directions as they drove further along. She took in the ornate Victorian clock tower, and the sailing boats in the bay, and the brightly painted beach huts along the shingle shore. There were the plaintive cries of seagulls, and a distant sweep of green fields stretching to the sea.

'Well, that's it,' Piers said, coming to the end of the coastal road. 'What would you like to do now?'

'Could we go for a walk?' she appealed. 'Can you spare the time?'

'Sure—we can leave the car here. A walk will do us good.'

He found a convenient space on the seafront and they strolled back towards the esplanade, pausing here and there to look out at the sea, or to watch some late water-skiers, or to admire the gardens.

'Oh, it's a dear little place.' Christina pushed back her hair, blown about by the breeze. 'I don't quite know what I was expecting, but this is it—the English seaside—except where's the sand? I remember making sand-pies somewhere.'

'You'd have to go further round the coast for that,' Piers told her.

'And the sea—it's so placid!' She leaned against the low wall, looking out at a tall-masted yacht riding the gentle swell.

'To be precise, it's really the Thames estuary still, and it's not always as calm as this, I can assure you.'

She breathed deeply of the buoyant atmosphere and passed her tongue over her lips. 'I can taste the salt, anyway,' she said, gazing out over dancing water, her eyes radiant.

Leaning beside her, against the sea-wall, Piers also relaxed as he savoured the tranquil ambience. He too was a little wind-blown, his rich dark hair breaking into wayward curls. Presently, with the sun beginning to set and the light to fade, he asked, 'Well, had enough of this yet?'

'OK,' she said reluctantly. 'I suppose there's not much more we could see tonight. . .'

'And you'll be coming again when you make contact with your relatives, won't you?' Piers put a hand lightly across her shoulders. 'Don't know about you, but I'm ravenous. Let's go and find that grub.'

It was the first time he had actually touched her, deliberately. Christina felt an intense thrill in the pit of her stomach and an odd tightness in her throat. All the same, she wished she were not finding it so enjoyable. He led her across the road on leaving the seafront and, sauntering back towards the town, they found an attractive pub, where they ordered from the wide menu chalked up on a blackboard.

'Oysters!' Piers exclaimed. 'They're the local delicacy—caught not far from here. Like to try some?'

She shook her head and shuddered. 'They look horribly gristly things to me. I'll stick with the melon. How about you?'

He laughed softly. 'I'd better stick with melon, too. Oysters are supposed to be an aphrodisiac.'

'Oh, is that what they're supposed to be?' Christina grinned. 'I'd have to be really, *really* desperate to try them.'

'Have you ever been—I mean, really desperate—or thought that you were?' His eyes, meeting hers, were enquiring, but then he raised an excusing hand. 'No, don't answer that. I shouldn't have asked. My trouble is I have this insatiable curiosity about people. Or nosiness, some people might call it.'

They were seated and eating their melon before she decided to satisfy him on that score. 'To put you straight,' she said, looking at him with amusement, 'don't worry—I didn't leave Australia with a broken heart.'

He smiled, but suddenly became more serious. 'I thought you might like to know, Christina, that young Sophie Branch told me talking with you had helped her more than anyone.'

Her mouth opened in surprise. True, she had always tried to be supportive when dealing with the girl, but hadn't realised that something of her philosophy had got through. 'I'm amazed. Mostly I let her do the talking. I hardly said anything at all,' she replied. 'All the same, privately I thought she was well out of a relationship with that smoothie.'

'I dare say she sensed your sympathy,' Piers remarked. 'I did just wonder if you'd had a similar experience?'

'*Me*? Good heavens, no. But I did have a friend who got involved with a married man—I vowed I'd never make the same mistake.'

Piers laughed. 'I'd say you know how many beans make five, Miss Linden.'

'So, now I've put your mind at rest, may I please concentrate on the rest of my meal without further inquisition?' Christina smiled sweetly, playing up to his idea of her as cool and self-possessed. If only he knew how wrong he was at this particular moment.

'Is that what it seemed like?' He controlled a grin. 'Take it as a compliment that I'm intrigued to know what makes you tick. So many pretty faces have nothing behind them.'

To her great annoyance she felt herself blushing. 'Perhaps it's my turn to ask the questions now,' she said with as much self-assurance as she could muster.

The waitress arriving with their main meal saved him the trouble of answering and their conversation returned to safer ground.

'You haven't been to one of our monthly ward meetings yet, have you?' Piers mentioned. 'Lately they haven't been very constructive—mostly turning into people airing their grievances. There's one fixed for Wednesday. I hope you'll try and come. It would be interesting to have a new slant on things.'

'Well, I've no moans so far, except my pet hate.'

He frowned. 'Your pet hate? What's that?'

'Oh, this putting men and women in the same ward, undivided. I think it's atrocious.'

'Do you think people really mind that much?' Piers queried. 'When people are sick, so long as they're being properly cared for, surely that's all that matters?' he asserted. 'They have their bed-curtains for privacy.'

Christina gave a resigned sigh. 'Only a man could be so insensitive.' She shook a finger at him. 'Listen, sport, personal delicacy might not matter to the male of the species, but, sick or not, most women care about the face they present to the world. They might not want strange guys to see them going to sleep in curlers and face cream.' She could see he was having a hard job keeping a straight face. 'OK,' she went on, 'you might think that's a frivolous argument, but morale plays a big part in patients' well-being. Besides, lots of older people are quite shy—both men and women.'

He sucked in his cheeks in an attempt at looking contrite. 'Didn't I say it would be good to have a fresh angle on things? Well, we won't pre-empt the meeting. That's the kind of thing you could bring up there. I'll get coffee—and then I wondered if you might like to sus out your aunt's house while we're here, so that you know your whereabouts?'

The same idea had been lurking at the back of her brain, but she hadn't liked to suggest it. 'Oh, that would be terrific, Piers,' she agreed. 'You're sure you don't mind? I do seem to be taking up an awful lot of your time.'

'Never leave a job half done is my motto. So long as you've got the address I can find it. A pity I can't produce the relatives.'

Christina's smile had an anxious edge. 'I only hope they'll be pleased to see me when we do meet. I'm beginning to wonder if I ought to have warned them I was coming—not sprung a surprise like this. Justin warned me his mum's apt to flap...and she is asthmatic.'

'Don't worry about it. I'm sure you'll be a very nice surprise,' Piers said comfortingly.

Darkness had fallen by the time they had finished their meal. It was a fair distance back to the car. He took her hand as they crossed the road, and then as quickly released it as though he was afraid of his action being misconstrued. Christina smiled to herself. Piers was that sort of man, she thought, naturally attentive to women. It was too bad the unfortunate secretary had read more into it.

They walked in companionable silence, listening to the soft slap of water against stones. Reaching the BMW, he switched on the inside light and pulled a gazetteer from the map pocket. Together they studied a local plan and found the required road.

'Right, that seems easy enough to find—and it's not far out of our way,' Piers said cheerfully.

Leaving the now quiet high street, they turned into a residential area of well-lit, tree-lined avenues with pleasing homes set well back from the road.

'This should be it.' He took a left turn. 'Which way do the numbers run—can you see?'

She peered out to look at gateposts. 'Even numbers this side—there's number ten. We want thirty.'

Slowly they travelled a few yards further along, then Piers drew the car to a quiet stop. 'Oh!' he said. 'Do you see what I see?'

Christina stopped searching for numbers and followed his gaze. What she saw, by the light of the street-lamp, was a familiar red sports car drawn up at the kerbside. The girl getting out of it on the passenger side had a cloud of long brown hair. The man whose arm went around her as he ushered her through the front gate of the house opposite was, without doubt, Christina's cousin Justin. 'Oh!' she said.

'Exactly!' Piers gave a short laugh. 'Your cousin doesn't know my car—and I don't think Donna noticed us. Not that I'd mind being seen with you,' he hastened to add, 'but I wouldn't like her to think I'm invading her space.'

'No, of course not,' Christina murmured. 'Well, I shan't let on that we were here.'

'Thanks. I'd rather not get involved with Donna's private affairs.'

He reversed the car and they began the journey back towards Canterbury. Passing through quiet countryside and scattered hamlets, at first they both spoke little, busy with their own thoughts. Presently, when they had come within sight of the city, with glimpses of the cathedral tower etched against the night sky, Piers became more talkative.

'This evening turned out vastly different from my expectations,' he confessed amiably. 'Thanks for your company, Christina. It's been—er—stimulating, to say the least.'

She looked at him with a pucker between her brows. 'How do you mean?'

'Well, seeing this corner of England through the eyes of a newcomer, for one thing, getting a new feminine viewpoint on this and that for another. Perhaps we should do this again some time.'

They were now approaching the hospital and he pulled into a lay-by to allow an ambulance right of way. He didn't start up again immediately. Instead he stretched expansively and ran his fingers through his hair, giving a deep sigh.

'May I tell you something?' Turning to look at her, he went on, 'Or perhaps you've already heard—about this girl who infringed on my life—overdosed and died because I didn't return her feelings?'

'Yes,' Christina admitted, 'I kind of gathered you'd been involved in some sort of catastrophe.'

'It made the headlines around here about eighteen months ago.' Piers leaned his elbow on the steering-wheel and his chin on his fist, and gazed into space. 'One of the secretaries, it was—she decided she was in love with me. God knows why. It wasn't a two-way thing, although I did have time for her because she was an excellent typist. It all started with me taking her out to dinner after she did a rush job for me, staying late to finish it. Then we got together at hospital socials—things like that—nothing really intimate. But she obviously got the wrong impression. She began to pester me, turned up at my flat—wouldn't leave me alone. In the end I had to spell it out to her that I didn't feel the same way. And she damn well OD'd!' He thumped his fist on the steering-wheel. 'Such a terrible waste of a life.'

Christina searched for the right thing to say. 'Oh, dear! That must have been really ghastly for you. Maybe she didn't mean it—perhaps she hoped she'd be found before it was too late. . .'

'Tactics which backfired, you mean? You could be right. But I often wonder if I was in any way to blame. Though I swear I never deliberately misled her about my feelings towards her. So that's my sorry tale, Christina.' His mouth twisted ruefully.

She shook her head, wanting to sympathise but at a loss to know how. 'In the end we're all responsible for our own actions, so you shouldn't feel guilty.' She paused. 'Best to try and put it behind you. I dare say you've come to the rescue of a good many others since then. Take Sophie, for instance. She was one of the luckier ones.'

He drew a deep breath and straightened up.

'I suppose what I've actually been trying to say, Christina, is that romance is a non-starter where I'm concerned, for the foreseeable future. No offence, but *please* don't read anything into the fact that we happened to spend this evening together, will you? I've enjoyed it—but all I can offer anyone is friendship. OK?'

She laughed. 'You needn't worry about me, Piers, I'm no clinging vine. I was just very grateful for the ride tonight.'

He patted his chest in extravagant relief. 'Thank you for understanding. I have to think twice before even smiling at a girl these days.' Starting up the car again, he went on, 'Now, where can I take you—is it the nurses' home?'

She nodded. 'Yes, if that's all right. Or I can walk when we get to the hospital.'

'Now why should you want to do that?' he demanded.

She hesitated. 'I—I just thought you might prefer not. . .'

'Not to be seen delivering you?' With a wry smile he drove on. 'I'm not quite that paranoid!'

They made the last part of the journey in silence. It was after eleven when he pulled up outside the hostel, where he deliberately alighted and came round to her side of the car.

'Pleasant dreams,' he said. 'Goodnight!'

'Goodnight, and thanks.' With a quiet smile she took the polite hand he offered. It was all very decorous and in a few moments he was gone.

Christina ran up to her room, glad to meet no one on the way. Her heart was pounding as she stripped off her sweatshirt and jeans. Sitting at the dressing-table in her towelling robe, she sought to calm down by putting a brush through her tousled fair hair. Her cheeks were pink and the grey-blue eyes that looked back at her were lustrous but solemn. 'Where do we go from here?' she pondered aloud. As far as Piers was concerned—nowhere. He had made that very plain. At least they understood each other, which would make working relations simpler. And tonight's conversation only underlined what she already knew. Giving way to any affectionate feelings she might harbour towards Piers Conrad would be a waste of good emotions. It would be as well for her to remember that.

CHAPTER FIVE

THE day of the ward meeting which Piers had mentioned to Christina duly arrived. It was timed to begin at nine p.m. to give both shifts the opportunity of being there. It also happened to be the start of Christina's days off. The night before, out of the blue, her friend Penny had telephoned from London. Wasn't it time she came up to town so that they could catch up with each other's news? Penny had said. Their spare room was ready and waiting.

'Well, I'd really love to, Pen,' Christina returned, 'but there's this wretched ward meeting tomorrow night. I half promised the medical reg I'd be there, which rather cramps my style.'

'Come for the day, then,' her friend persuaded. 'I've got these two complimentary matinée tickets for *Joseph* at The London Palladium, and Matt can't make it. You'll have oodles of time to get back to your meeting. It only takes just over an hour to Victoria, doesn't it? I'll meet you there, say, elevenish, and we can do the shops and have some lunch. The show starts at two-thirty, so you could be getting a train back to Canterbury in plenty of time for your meeting.'

The prospect of seeing the West End show was too good to miss. Accordingly, the following morning Christina was up early and catching a bus to the railway station. Some time later the two friends were greeting each other as planned at the Victoria terminal. Time simply evaporated as they talked over coffee, and then lunch, exchanging confidences.

'Oh, it's great to have a natter with you again,' Christina said. 'Everyone at North Downs has been really friendly, but it's not the same as talking to someone you know.'

Penny shook her red curls. 'Why did you have to bury yourself down there, for heaven's sake?'

'You know why. I needed to find my roots. Besides, you've got Matt here, and I dare say you'll both go back to Oz eventually, won't you?'

'Mmm—maybe. It depends what's in it over here for Matt, I suppose,' her friend pondered. 'Where he goes, I go.'

'Still love's young dream, is it?'

'You bet!' Penny sighed. 'When there's the time, and no other predatory females around. But that applies wherever you are. So how about these relatives of yours—have you had the grand reunion yet?'

'Nope—except with my cousin Justin, who nearly died on me. Boy, was that a close shave!'

Penny chuckled. 'Yes, so you said. Back home we worry about spiders lurking in shoes, et cetera, and over here a little old bee could wipe you out.'

A few hours later they had been to the theatre and were hastening back to Victoria for Christina to catch her train. They arrived with barely five minutes to spare.

'Bye!' Penny said. They exchanged quick hugs at the ticket barrier. 'Keep in touch!'

'Will do. Thanks for a terrific day.' Christina waved and hurried along the platform with her shopping bags. Spotting a compartment not entirely full, she jumped in, slung her packages on to the rack and gratefully sank on to an available corner seat by a window. Carriage doors slammed and the train slowly moved out of the station. It was six-forty, she saw, glancing at her wristwatch. They were due back in Canterbury just after eight—plenty of time to make the meeting. Not that it was obligatory to attend, only she wouldn't like Piers Conrad to think her uncaring.

The train sped merrily on its way, with only the occasional stop. Gazing out at the passing evening countryside, with catchy tunes from the musical still lingering in her head, Christina was in a philosophical mood. Oh, yes, London was an exciting place, but she was happy to be going back to Canterbury and North Downs Hospital. The fact that it had been her mother's background gave her a warm glow. She had a feeling that this was where she belonged.

The train coming to an unprecedented halt just outside Faversham interrupted her reverie. Five minutes later there was a crackly apology over the loudspeaker, along with the explanation that a signals failure further down the line was responsible for the delay.

Although she knew it was pointless to get exasperated, nevertheless Christina sat there and fidgeted, privately incensed with the railway for threatening her plans.

A fellow traveller in the seat opposite—a grey-haired man in a city suit—noted her impatience as she checked her watch yet again. 'Infuriating, isn't it?' he said.

'Yes, I have to get to a meeting at nine o'clock,' she explained. 'I'm not going to make it if they don't get a move on.'

'Too bad. Much further to go?'

'Canterbury,' she told him, 'and a short ride on from there.'

'Oh, wish I could help, but I'll be leaving the train at the next stop.' He put his head on one side, his expression quizzical. 'Forgive me, but haven't I seen you before?'

There was something vaguely familiar about him, now she thought about it. 'Have you? I don't know.' She wondered if he might perhaps have been visiting someone at the hospital. It served a wide area.

'Weren't you dining with a young man recently—and he collapsed in the restaurant?'

'Oh!' Christina smiled. 'Yes, were you there?'

He nodded. 'It was my son who came to your aid. I heard your friend made a good recovery.'

'You're Dr Conrad's father!' Christina exclaimed, suddenly catching on. 'Now I can see the family likeness.' She laughed. 'Sorry, I was far too worried at the time to notice who else was there.'

Her fellow traveller leaned across to shake hands. 'John Conrad. So glad everything turned out all right.'

'I'm Christina Linden,' she said. 'You probably heard I'm a nurse at the hospital. Are you also a doctor?'

'Good gracious, no! But Piers' mother was a nurse. That's probably what motivated him.'

'He's the one who's expecting me at this meeting,' Christina said. 'My name will be mud if I don't get there.'

'Oh, dear! Well, I shall be your alibi,' Mr Conrad promised. 'Any trouble, you refer him to me. Of course, you met my stepdaughter, Donna,' he went on.

'Yes, although we haven't seen each other again since that day.'

'She's a nice lass, but I don't know that she's the stuff nurses are made of,' he mused.

'It takes time,' Christina said. Anxious not to be sounded out on the subject of Donna, she told him about her day in London and they carried on talking agreeably as the time slipped by.

Some twenty minutes later the train gave a sudden lurch forward and they were on their way again.

'Well, thank goodness for that,' she said. 'I may still make it, if I get a taxi at the other end.'

The train drew into Faversham station. John Conrad rose, gathered his briefcase from the overhead rack, wished her good luck in getting to the meeting, and said goodnight.

Within another fifteen minutes Christina was arriving at Canterbury. It was now ten minutes to nine. She felt extremely travel-worn and crumpled in the cream linen suit she had worn since early morning, but there was no time to go back to her room, leave her shopping and tidy up. She would have to go straight to the hospital.

Hurrying out of the station, she hailed a taxi and gave the driver instructions.

'You look a bit hot and bothered, love,' he observed while easing into the stream of traffic out of the city. 'Got someone sick at the hospital, have you?'

'No.' She grinned self-consciously. 'I work there—and I'm late for a meeting, that's all. Not my fault. The wretched train was late.'

'Oh! Not to worry, then. Not a capital offence, like, is it?' he joked.

'No,' she agreed. 'It's just that I wanted to make a good impression, being new.'

'Right-o, love. I'll do me best,' he promised.

It seemed they hit every red traffic-light on the route, but Christina saw sense in the cabbie's attitude. For goodness' sake, it was her days off, after all. And if it hadn't been for Piers and his wretched meeting she might have stayed the night in London with Penny. Deep down, though, she felt it was important to be there if she valued his good opinion.

It was ten minutes past the hour when the taxi drew up outside the main entrance to the hospital. Paying the fare, she thanked the driver for his efforts.

'You give 'em that smile, me dear, and you'll have 'em eating out of your hand in no time,' he declared. 'G'night!'

Hurrying in through the main doors, Christina darted down the corridor towards the medical wing.

Thankful to find a lift standing waiting, she took it to the second floor. Arriving, she flew along the passage until she came to the closed door of the staffroom, where she paused for breath before tapping a knock, opening it and looking in.

The room was quite full, people comfortably seated, some in everyday clothes and some in uniform. All eyes turned to look at her as she made her late entry. Catching Piers Conrad's eye, she was relieved to see that he appeared more curious than disapproving.

'So sorry to be late, Helen,' Christina said a little breathlessly. 'I've come back from London, and the train was held up. A signals failure, apparently.'

'You haven't missed anything important—we've only just started,' the sister said placidly. 'Find yourself a seat somewhere.'

Patrick pulled a chair forward into the circle between himself and a staff nurse she didn't know. Meanwhile Helen carried on going through the 'Update' book, asking for comments on various suggestions and complaints which had been put forward.

There were grumbles about stock cupboards being left untidy, and visitors not replacing chairs after use, and urinals being left by the bedside without covers. Patrick said some nurses were still lending equipment to other wards and not getting a signature, so how were they to check up on supplies? Someone else complained about visitors sitting on beds.

'Surely that's an infection risk, and it can't be comfortable for the patient,' she said.

'We-ell, if this were an ideal world, we'd all be abiding by the rules,' Helen observed with a sigh. 'Hasn't anyone anything encouraging to say?'

'Yes, I have,' Rachel piped up happily. 'You all know Thelma, my hemiplegic patient; well, she's getting some movement in her left side at last—and today she started to write messages on a notepad, using her good hand. Isn't that great? We can begin to communicate.'

Piers Conrad, who had been quiet until then, smiled. 'Very rewarding,' he said. 'We're trying to get her a place at a rehabilitation centre, where her progress should be even better.'

'Her parents should be pleased about that—if it's not too far away,' Helen put in. 'They're not too happy about her being in a mixed ward.'

'I think Christina has views on mixed wards,' Piers remarked from the depths of his easy-chair. 'Perhaps she'd care to enlarge on that.'

Christina cast a baleful glance towards the registrar. She was still feeling somewhat rushed and breathless—not in the least like grabbing the spotlight and holding forth. 'Well. . .' she hesitated '. . .I *was* rather surprised to see male and female patients put together in one ward,' she said. 'I'd never experienced that kind of thing before. Maybe divided into four- or six-bedded bays, but not in a Nightingale-type ward like this.'

'I agree,' put in the nurse beside her. 'My mother didn't like it. Bad enough being in hospital in the first place, she said, without totally losing one's dignity.'

'Would you rather we sent people away, while beds in some wards lay empty?' Piers asked. 'Come on, we'd have the world at our heels if we did that.'

'A little bit of imagination and I'm sure it could be sorted out,' Christina argued. 'It wouldn't cost the earth for some extra curtaining and a few more bed-rails.'

'OK, you work out a plan and let me have it,' Piers retorted, an ironic twist to his mouth. 'I'm prepared to put it to the committee and see what they say. But if it means fewer beds in the same space, forget it!'

Patrick laughed. 'That'll teach you to open your mouth, my girl. You've got yourself a job now.'

'All right, I will,' she declared with a sideways glance

at the registrar. He thought he had put her on the spot, but she'd show him what was possible—she hoped!

They left the vexed subject of ward problems and got on with talking about the centenary celebrations in just over two weeks' time. Helen had the programme of events dreamed up by the Society of Friends. At the local showground there were to be displays by the police and the fire and rescue services, music by a military band, and side-stalls by various voluntary organisations. Wanted from the wards were teams for a knock-out competition to take place throughout the day, and entries for a car treasure hunt, the winning team to be awarded the prize of their choice for their ward. There was much laughter as people grew enthusiastic about whatever appealed to them most.

'I'll pin a sheet up in my office and anyone interested in taking part, write your names down and I'll do my best with the off-duty,' Helen promised. 'Let's call it a day and have some coffee now, shall we?'

Christina jumped up to help with the drinks, handing them round while someone else poured. When all were served she went back to rescue her parcels from where she had dumped them on the floor beside her chair. Patrick had moved away and was talking to Helen. Christina was about to speak to the staff nurse alongside her when Piers Conrad came to claim her attention.

'Spent all your money?' he asked lightly.

'Almost. Oh, and you'll never guess who I travelled home with tonight!' she said.

'Guessing games were never my forte,' he returned. 'Your cousin, was it?'

'No—your father.'

His eyes widened in surprise. 'How did you know each other?'

'Well, it was he who recognised me, actually, but I don't think he would have spoken if the train hadn't been held up. He promised to be my alibi if I didn't make the meeting,' she added, smiling. 'He got out at Faversham.'

Piers nodded. 'When he's going to be late he prefers to drive up to there from Broadstairs,' he began.

At that point Amy Gillow came in search of him, wanting advice on a patient. With a resigned sigh Piers excused himself and went with her to the ward.

The heavily built girl sitting next to Christina decided to introduce herself. 'I'm Karen Hill,' she said. 'I've been off sick. Only came back today.'

'Oh, hi!' Christina returned with a friendly smile to the straight-faced staff nurse. 'Glad you're better.'

'You're new on this ward, aren't you?' Karen said.

'Yes, this is my fourth week. I'm Christina Linden.'

'You seem very friendly with Piers Conrad,' Karen remarked pointedly. 'Did you know him before you came to this hospital?'

'No—we just seem to have had a lot to do with each other, that's all.'

'Oh! Only I should watch yourself with that one,' the staff nurse warned. 'You won't get anywhere with him. He's a workaholic—no time for girlfriends.'

Christina smiled. 'It's OK, it didn't take me long to find that out.' Privately she wondered if Karen had at some time been rebuffed. She went on, 'I think they really missed not having you around on the ward.'

'Yeah!' Karen raised her eyes to heaven. 'When you're not there they realise who does the work.'

The meeting had now broken up and most people were leaving, but it was still nagging away in Christina's mind what she had undertaken to do. 'Helen,' she said, going to the sister, 'do we have a tape measure anywhere?'

'Sure—one in the desk drawer. What do you want it for?' Helen asked.

'I just thought I might take the opportunity

to measure the width of a bed—and the space between them.'

Helen pealed with laughter. 'Oh, come on, surely you didn't take Piers seriously?'

'I certainly did,' Christina returned. 'I'd like to prove my point. The night nurses won't mind me creeping about for a bit, will they?'

'Shouldn't think so, so long as you don't disturb the patients.' The sister was obviously highly amused by Christina's attitude. 'I'm away to my bed,' she declared; 'they've had their pennyworth out of me today,' and padded off on her crêpe-soled shoes.

In the empty office Christina found the tape measure where Helen had said it would be, after which she went along to the darkened ward to check with the night staff that they had no objections to her being there. Luckily the nurse she found locking away the drugs trolley was someone she'd had dealings with.

'Fine by me,' she said, when put in the picture. 'Dr Conrad and the HO are down the ward, checking up on Mr Chalice, but you won't disturb them, will you?'

'No, and I shouldn't be more than ten minutes anyway. Thanks,' Christina murmured. 'I'll be quiet as a mouse!'

Armed with notebook and ballpoint she set about her task. Firstly she measured the overall width and length of the nearest bed, and then the distance between beds. Then she stood for a few minutes, letting her eyes take in other details such as access to the sluice and the doctors' handbasin, bed lights and piped oxygen facilities. It simplified matters that there was no fixed central table and that the patients' bathrooms and toilets were off the passage outside. Having thus memorised the layout as best she could, Christina slipped her notebook into her jacket pocket, said goodnight to the staff nurse, returned the tape measure to where it belonged and collected her shopping from where she had left it in the meeting-room.

Her head full of facts and figures, she strolled thoughtfully towards the lift. As she waited for it to arrive, her heart suddenly began to quicken as she saw the tall, athletic figure of Piers striding along the lighted corridor. Hands thrust into his trouser pockets, he continued coming in her direction. The silver lift doors slid back. She stepped in, but common courtesy dictated that she should hold the lift, in case he needed it. He apparently did, stepping in beside her with an appreciative smile.

'Thanks for waiting.' Eyeing her parcels, he went on jokingly, 'So at last you can go home and gloat over all the goodies you bought.'

'To have a much needed shower, you mean,' she returned. 'Gosh, I feel so tacky. I haven't so much as put a comb through my hair since I set out before nine this morning.'

He made a thorough inspection of her tumbled fair hair, her glowing complexion and wide grey-blue eyes. Which had her heart beating even more frantically. 'As far as I can tell, you've come through in good order,' he said, 'and I respect your efforts to get back in time for the meeting. I know it's a nuisance if you happen to have other plans.'

They had by now arrived at the ground floor. The doors slid back. He stood aside to let her pass. In her confusion she dropped the plastic carrier containing her new summer sandals. Both stooped to pick it up, and their faces brushed.

'Ouch!' she exclaimed as his chin rubbed her cheek. 'You need a shave.'

'Sorry about that. I've been going flat out since early this morning as well,' he remarked with a wry smile. 'Shall I carry this for you? I'll walk you to the nurses' home—I feel like a breath of fresh air—and you can tell me what's going on in your busy world.'

Already his deep, thrilling voice was turning her present world upside-down. But with warnings coming from outsiders like Karen, as well as himself, she'd be an idiot if she let his bedevilling charm sweep away her sanity.

'What's going on in my world seems to have been overtaken by what's going on in yours,' she retorted blithely, 'now that you've lumbered me with this ward-reorganising job.'

They left the hospital buildings and he chuckled as they stepped out, side by side, into the still night. 'As Patrick said, that will teach you, my girl. However, if it bothers you, don't worry. It wasn't an order.'

'Now he tells me!' she said. 'All the same, I intend to see what I can do.'

'That sounds like fighting talk,' he returned.

Lighted at infrequent intervals, the road to the nurses' hostel was lined on either side with great banks of rhododendron bushes. Some were just breaking into flower and the lamplight shone mystically on the pearly-pink blooms.

Admiring their ghostly beauty, Christina sighed with pleasure. 'I'm falling more and more in love with this countryside,' she said.

'Are we going to have you for keeps, then?' Piers asked in a teasing manner. 'I thought you might have been disillusioned after seeing that pebbly beach at Herne Bay.'

'Every place has its character. I suppose it's the people you associate with it who make it special, or otherwise,' she said.

'I see. So you're reserving judgement until you've met your kith and kin, right?'

'Maybe.' She smiled to herself, knowing that whatever happened the evening she had spent with Piers in the small holiday town had cast a magic aura over it which she would never forget. To be honest, even walking beside him like this, without touching, had the power to kick-start erotic feelings within her.

They reached the hostel. He waited, holding her parcels while she searched for her key to open the front door. She looked up at him, her eyes starry, as they were about to part. 'Thank you for coming,' she said.

He stood for a moment, not speaking, simply looking at her with that rare, disarming smile which had won him many a battle over the years. Her heart began to stampede as she wondered what might be in his mind. Then he merely lifted his hand and ruffled her hair. 'My pleasure. Enjoy your shower. Goodnight,' he said, fairly briskly, and he walked away.

Christina climbed the stairs to her room, her face flushed, startled by her own weakness. Oh, God! She had almost willed him to want to kiss her. How could she have been such an idiot? Face facts, she reminded herself. Maybe he *was* attracted to her, ever so slightly, but that was as far as it went—he had been quick to tell her as much. Anyway, she hadn't come to England looking for a lover, had she?

When she arrived at her room, written on the notepad pinned to her door was the message, 'Justin phoned. Please ring him a.s.a.p.' Well, at least that was something to take her mind off the devastating registrar. Going into her room to leave her shopping, she looked at the time. It was now well past eleven—a bit late for making phone calls when you didn't know a person's habits. However, she decided to risk it.

Searching out some coins, Christina went along to the payphone in the corridor and dialled Justin's number. It rang several times before he answered.

'Justin? Hello! Just got your message,' she said. 'Sorry it's so late. Hope you weren't in bed.'

He laughed. 'That's OK. I just called to tell you that my folks are home. I've broken the news that you're here, and they're looking forward to seeing you when you're free. Give them a ring some time—and if you'll let me know when you can make it I'll try and run you over there. All right?'

'Oh, yes, Justin, that would be great,' she said. 'I bet they were surprised, weren't they?'

'You can say that again!' Her cousin laughed. 'It was a good thing we met up first, though—Mum nearly blew a fuse, as I thought she might. Still, I calmed her down—told her what a sweetie you are. Look, Chris, why not call me at work tomorrow? I'm—er—rather tied up at the moment.'

Christina heard the sound of a soft giggle and her cousin murmuring, 'Shush, Donna.'

'Oh, sorry,' she said, 'only your message sounded urgent. Anyway, thanks for phoning. Yes, I'll ring you in the morning. Bye!'

Going back to her room, she had a vague feeling of unease. So, something was really cooking between those two? She hoped Donna knew what she was doing.

Throwing off her day clothes and getting into her bathrobe and slippers, Christina gathered up her towel and toilet things and went along to the communal bathrooms. They were all occupied, but after she had waited a few minutes it was Judy who finally emerged from one of them, towelling her short dark hair.

'Hi!' Judy greeted her cheerfully. 'I knocked on your door earlier. Wondered if you wanted to come out for some grub, but you weren't there.'

'No, days off,' Christina explained. 'I met a friend in London, and then I dashed back for a ward meeting which went on forever.'

Judy raised her eyes heavenwards. 'They often do, and don't get anywhere. Still, it's as well to show willing.'

Christina smiled. 'Yeah, that's what I thought.' It

brought back to mind her self-imposed task, but she didn't feel inclined to talk about it at that moment. 'It was mainly about the centenary celebrations,' she said. 'Looks like being a fun weekend. How's the hot water?'

'Fine! That's the only good thing about this dump—no worries about getting a bath.'

Judy went on her way and Christina decided on a long soak instead of a shower, but instead of relaxing her it only served to activate her brain. She lay there visualising the rearrangement of beds and furniture and hoping she could make it look good so that the powers-that-be would see the possibilities. It would be best to get hold of some graph paper, she thought. Plotting it out to scale shouldn't be too difficult since she knew the number of beds and the overall size of them, et cetera.

Her thoughts came back again to Justin and Donna, and inevitably to her aunt and uncle, now returned from their holiday. Just as well she had no other plans for tomorrow. They *might* suggest seeing her straight away, unless they had jet-lag.

The following morning Christina was up early and pondering when would be the best time to ring Herne Bay. She decided to leave it until midday, which would give her the morning to concentrate on the ward plan. Searching through some nursing records among her belongings, she found a few unused sheets of the desired graph paper and set to work. Several mugs of coffee later and the arrangement of beds was accomplished to her satisfaction. The only snag was likely to be the individual bed lights, radio points and piped oxygen. But for goodness' sake, Piers couldn't expect her to be a technician as well, she thought. Someone else would have to work out details like that!

With a sigh of satisfaction she tucked her neatly

drawn chart into an envelope and put it in her shoulder-bag, ready to hand over to the registrar at the first opportune moment.

By now it was twelve o'clock and time she made that vital phone call. Excitement grew in her like a bottled fizzy drink vigorously shaken. Her fingers were all thumbs as she searched out the telephone number before going along to the payphone in the corridor.

It was a rumbling male voice which answered her call. 'Henry Wells,' he announced.

'Hello!' she returned. 'This is Christina—would you be my uncle Henry?'

'Christina!' her uncle boomed. 'Yes, my dear, that's me all right. Justin told us you'd blown in. How are you, love?' He sounded really delighted and soon they were chatting like old friends.

He wanted to know of her activities to date and she asked about their holiday. As the minutes passed she wondered when he might hand her over to Aunt Beth, but he carried on talking endlessly. Presently he said, 'Well, when can we expect to see you, dear? I'm afraid I must ask you to leave it for a few days—your aunt has come back with a shocking cold. Gone to her chest—she's had to take to her bed for a bit.'

'Oh, dear! Sorry to hear that,' Christina sympathised. 'Do give her my love and say to look after herself. In any case, I don't have any more off-duty for a while—but I could perhaps come out one evening, when I'm on an early.'

'Or I could come and take you out for a meal,' he suggested. 'I'm busting to see you. I was very fond of your mother, you know.'

She gave him her telephone number, and they left it that they'd be in touch when it was more convenient.

Well, that's that! Christina thought, glad to have made contact at last. Her uncle sounded terrific, really welcoming, but she was still in the dark as to how her aunt Beth would receive her. What had been the rift between the two sisters remained a mystery to Christina and she had no wish to go rattling skeletons.

CHAPTER SIX

ON FRIDAY Christina returned to work after her days off. Going on at midday, she had missed the morning doctors' rounds and there was no immediate chance to give her ward plan to Piers, much to her disappointment. Having battled with it, she was anxious to hand it over as soon as possible.

With the oncoming staff gathered in the office, Patrick gave his ward report. 'No evidence of malignancy in any of Mr Taylor's tests,' he said. 'His haemoglobin's back to normal, so he's for discharge tomorrow, on cimetidine.' His eyes lifted towards Christina. 'There'll be a letter for his GP and he'll need an outpatient appointment in four weeks.'

Karen Hill, being the senior nurse on duty, scribbled pretentiously in her notebook. Patrick gave her a sideways enquiring glance. 'You needn't bother yourself with that, Karen. Christina will do the necessary, won't you?'

'Yes, of course.' Christina wondered why the comment.

'When I'm in charge I like to keep my finger on the pulse of things,' Karen returned primly.

'We are trying to practise primary nursing here, remember,' Patrick pointed out. He carried on with his report. 'We'll be losing Thelma tomorrow. She's for transfer to the rehabilitation centre. Make sure you speak to her parents about that this afternoon, Rachel—just in case they haven't been told.'

'Will do. That's come at rather a good time for me,' the third-year said. 'I'm leaving this ward after today—going into my last study block on Monday.'

'Oh, so you are. Helen went through your report, didn't she?' The charge nurse gave Rachel a friendly grin. 'We shall miss you. You've done a good job here. Well, to get on, Mr Chalice is rather poorly.' This time he addressed his remarks to Enid, a mature enrolled nurse who was always obliging and reliable. 'Seems to have a general infection and is a bit confused—his temp was thirty-eight plus this morning. Dr Conrad put him on amoxycillin q.d. and ordered another blood test. Thinks it could be a prostate problem. He's to be seen by the surgeon.' He turned a page. 'Then we have Lucy Hadlow, aged thirty, married—no children, query Graves's disease. Admitted yesterday. She's to have the usual thyroid function tests to confirm thyrotoxicosis, but there doesn't seem much doubt. . .'

'Oh, yes, I heard about her,' Christina put in, not thinking.

'How was that?' Karen promptly enquired.

'Er—I just happened to know someone who knew her,' Christina explained tactfully.

'Right, then, how about you taking her on?' Patrick said. 'Piers wants her handled with kid gloves. She's hyper-nervous. And Karen will be far too busy to tackle it, won't you?'

The irony in his tone was totally lost on the staff nurse. She shrugged. 'Well, you know how it is. With the best will in the world, I've only got one pair of hands.'

Patrick smiled wryly. 'OK. Back to Mrs Hadlow. She had a dose of radioactive iodine, orally, at ten, and they'll be coming to take blood later this afternoon.' Closing his notebook, he slipped his ballpoint into his breast pocket. 'Don't forget to remind the night staff we need a sleeping pulse at two a.m. for her, will you, Christina?' He went off duty and the other nurses scattered to their tasks.

Christina first went to make the acquaintance of her

new patient. In the high-dependency area she found a thin, dark-haired woman who would have been pretty but for the protruding, anxious brown eyes and visible smooth swelling around her neck. Even wearing just a flimsy sleeveless nightdress and with only a sheet for covering, her skin looked moist and clammy.

'Hello, Lucy!' Christina introduced herself with a bright smile. 'I'm going to be looking after you today. I'll be coming to have a proper chat as soon as I've done one or two essentials.' She paused. 'You're looking a bit warm, love. . .'

'I know—isn't it awful? I seem to sweat as soon as I move,' the girl said, her voice husky. 'I can hardly wear anything less—I feel half-naked as it is, with all these guys around.'

Christina smiled. 'Oh, don't worry about them. They're far too concerned with their own problems to be looking at you.' She checked Lucy's pulse and found it woefully rapid, although her temperature was normal. 'I'll get an electric fan,' she went on. 'That might make you feel more comfortable. Are you expecting visitors this afternoon?'

'Yes, my parents, I hope, although they do have to come a fair distance,' the woman said breathily. 'My husband won't be here till this evening. He works in London.'

Lucy seemed very anxious to talk and confide her fears, telling Christina that it was loss of weight, tiredness and two missed periods which had first sent her to see her GP. 'I hoped I was pregnant, but no such luck,' she sighed.

'Well, perhaps when we've sorted you out it will happen,' Christina said sympathetically. 'I'll go and get that fan—and a bowl of water so that you can freshen up. The doctor wants you to stay in bed for the time being. You need to rest as much as possible.'

After getting the bowl of water she drew the curtains

around the bed, placed the patient's toilet bag and towel within easy reach and left her to carry on.

Enid asked for her help in getting Mr Chalice into a chair and changing his bottom sheet. 'He's so apologetic about being a nuisance, although I keep telling him not to worry. He's a nice old boy,' she said. 'Hope he's going to be all right.'

'He should improve once the antibiotics take over,' Christina reasoned. 'What would we do without them?'

'Yes, I know.' Enid shook her head, pushing the linen bin down the ward. 'Must've been frustrating in the old days when there wasn't a lot they could do to fight infection.'

Drawing him into their conversation as much as possible, they made the patient tidy and comfortable in a chair and pulled his bed-table to hand.

Their work finished, Christina stripped off her plastic apron and washed her hands at a basin. 'Where did Helen put that list, Enid?' she asked. 'You know, the one for volunteers for that knock-out team for the centenary.'

'Oh, that. It's been taken down now. They had enough names.'

'Oh, pity. I thought it sounded a hoot. Wouldn't have minded taking part,' Christina said.

Enid grinned. 'You may be well out of it, judging by some of the capers they dream up for these things. Personally I'm happy to be a spectator—apart from putting our dog in the pooch-with-waggiest-tail contest.'

Amy Gillow, their diminutive house officer, came hurrying into the ward, her long white coat flapping around her ankles. 'Just made it!' she panted, checking her wristwatch. 'Piers said this blood sample from the thyrotoxic girl has to be taken precisely four hours after the oral iodine, and you know what he's like. Not around, is he?'

'No, we haven't seen him this afternoon,' Christina reassured her.

'Oh, good. Come with me while I do it, would you? Just in case there are any problems.'

'Sure,' Christina smiled. 'I'll get the necessary for you. I was just about to do her observations again.'

Later that afternoon, during her tea-break, Christina telephoned her cousin.

'Sorry about last night,' he said. 'I was just about to take my visitor back to her place. Anyway, I've spoken to Dad. He's busy tomorrow—got a wedding to cover. How are you fixed for Sunday?'

'On an early,' she told him, 'but I'll be free after four-thirty.'

'Great! I hoped you would be. Dad would like to take us out to dinner. Shall he pick you up where I did that time we first met?'

'Yes, that would be lovely, if it's no trouble. Will Aunt Beth be able to make it?' Christina asked.

'Sorry, no, she'll have to give this one a miss. Her chesty colds hang about.' He paused. 'Christina, I expect you've probably realised I'm seeing Donna. You wouldn't mind, would you, if I brought her along? I'd like Dad to meet her, and this would be a good chance, without it being too obvious.'

Christina smiled to herself. 'Fine by me, Justin. It'll even up the numbers, won't it? Sorry about Aunt Beth, though. Has she seen a doctor?'

'I don't know. Probably—she usually takes good care of herself.'

He didn't sound unduly concerned, so Christina said no more. Leaving it to Justin to tell her uncle that she would meet him on Sunday evening, as arranged, she went back to work.

During her absence Piers had arrived, bringing the urology consultant to see Mr Chalice. They were being fussily waited on by Karen.

'Where she sprang from goodness knows,' Enid said, her annoyance tempered with good humour. 'Suddenly there she was, snatching the case-notes out of my hands.'

'If she's that keen on running the show, why doesn't she apply for a sister's post somewhere?' Christina asked.

'Problems at home,' Enid told her. 'There's a little spastic sister. I've always counted my blessings that my kids are normal.'

'Oh, I see.' Christina was thoughtful, feeling more charitable towards the officious staff nurse. 'That could explain a lot. Maybe at home she has to take something of a back seat.'

Piers and the consultant left the ward together, deep in conversation, and Karen came bustling into the office with the case-notes, which she flung on the desk.

'As I thought,' she announced importantly. 'Mr Chalice does have an enlarged prostate. As soon as his infection clears up he'll be referred for tests and surgery. Enid, you can write that up, can't you?'

Christina left the two of them to sort it out. She stepped along the corridor in the hope that Piers was still about, but the doctor's office door stood open and the room was empty. For a moment she considered leaving her ward plan on the desk, but there was always the chance of it going astray. Besides, there were things she needed to explain to him. No, she had better give it to him personally. Perhaps he might be in again later.

However, day turned into night, the night nurses arrived and Christina went off duty, her ward plan still in her holdall. Barring emergency calls they were unlikely now to see any more of the registrar on the ward until after the weekend.

Deciding what to wear for her first meeting with her uncle Henry that Sunday was no easy choice for

Christina. First impressions were important. She longed to be accepted by her mother's family. She desperately wanted them to like her, to bury whatever differences there had been between the two sisters. Oh, what the hell? she finally thought after much agonising. If things didn't work out it wouldn't be through any lack of effort on her part.

Sunday evening saw her waiting outside the hostel as Justin had suggested. What had started off as a bright summer day was now overcast, and even in her neat turquoise blue suit, teamed with a primrose silk shirt, she felt a little shivery. Purposely ten minutes early so as not to keep her uncle waiting, she hovered from foot to foot, gazing in the direction of the car park, wishing it were tomorrow and that the initial meeting was behind her.

People and cars came and went. Her heart suddenly missed a beat when she recognised the white BMW which drew to a halt by the roadside in front of her. It was Piers! And she hadn't got that wretched ward plan with her or she might have handed it over.

The registrar alighted and sauntered towards her, incredibly heart-stopping, hands in the trouser pockets of his lightweight grey suit. 'Hello!' he said.

'Hello!' she returned, puzzled and ridiculously envious of whoever he might be calling for.

'Well, are you coming?' he asked, one eyebrow lifting equivocally.

She stared at him in total confusion.

'Hasn't anyone told you?' He gave a patient smile. 'That figures, if Donna had anything to do with it. It appears your aunt decided she was well enough to come and meet you tonight. Donna roped me in to escort you to make the numbers even.'

Christina was still trying to get her breath back as he led her to the car. 'Oh, gosh! Nice of you to agree, although it really wouldn't have mattered. Piers, I'm so sorry you keep getting mixed up in my affairs. Hope it didn't interfere with anything else you planned to do.'

'Nothing important.' He saw her into the car. 'Besides, this gives me the opportunity of seeing what young Donna's up to, among other things,' he added with a muted grin.

Christina's head was in a whirl. 'Life's full of surprises,' she said gaily. 'I don't know what kind of evening we're in for, but at least with more people present there shouldn't be too many awkward pauses.'

A small frown grew between his brows. 'Do I get the feeling you think it might be—difficult?'

Christina shrugged. 'Although it's family, it is unknown territory.'

'Come on, that's negative thinking,' he said. 'You started from the other side of the world with good intentions. If other people don't appreciate that, then they're not worth bothering with.'

She drew a deep breath. 'Thanks, Piers. I needed someone to tell me that. The trouble is, there was some kind of rift between my mother and her sister, but I never found out exactly why.'

'I did wonder if there might be a problem, by something you once said.' He threw her a sudden sideways smile. 'Don't worry about it. Play it by ear. I'll kick you under the table if I think your confidence is slipping.'

The country hotel chosen for their meeting was only a short ride from the hospital. Justin's red sports car was already in the car park when they arrived. Making for the cocktail lounge with Piers at her side, Christina was buoyed up with the comforting knowledge that she had an impressive escort, whatever else transpired. Being with the dynamic registrar seemed to lend her an inner strength.

Four pairs of eyes turned in their direction when Piers and Christina entered the lounge. Justin came striding forward with a kiss for her and a hearty handshake for Piers before leading them towards the elderly couple and Donna.

There was no waiting for an introduction to her uncle. A big, bluff man with a shock of iron-grey hair, 'My dear girl!' he exclaimed, seizing her in a vast hug and kissing her exuberantly. 'I'd have known you anywhere. You're the image of your mother at that age—isn't she, Beth?'

Christina's aunt, a middle-aged figure with dark curly hair and a pallid complexion, was standing back, waiting to be introduced. She turned her cheek when Christina went to embrace her affectionately. 'Don't want to give you my germs,' she said.

'Oh, never mind that. It's great of you to come.' Christina hugged her regardless. 'Are you really feeling better?'

'She's all right, aren't you, old girl?' Henry said. 'Expect it was a hangover from our flight home.'

With the rest of the courtesies observed, the small talk flowed politely as they sipped their drinks while waiting to be called to the dining-room.

'No floral arrangements here, thank goodness, eh, Christina?' Justin remarked with a light laugh.

'Why, what do you mean by that?' his mother wanted to know.

'I got stung by a bee while you were away, Mother. Apparently I've got an allergy to stings. These two saved my life.'

'Well, Piers may have done,' Christina smiled. 'Justin's luck was in that evening,' she told his parents, 'a doctor being on hand when he was needed.'

Seeing the blank astonishment on their faces, Donna was happy to fill them in with her version of events. 'It was *astounding*!' she exclaimed in her extravagant fashion. 'We were all in this restaurant, quietly having coffee at our separate tables, when there was this commotion over an insect buzzing around. We saw Justin get up as if to go to the cloakroom, then his legs just seemed to give out and he slithered to a heap on the carpet.'

Justin beamed at the registrar. 'So this is a double thank-you from me tonight—firstly that I'm here at all, and secondly because it introduced me to Donna.'

It was the first time Christina had seen Piers looking modestly embarrassed. He smiled. 'I've been cast in a few roles in my time,' he said, 'but a matchmaker—that's a new one.'

Christina's aunt tutted. 'Can't leave Justin for a moment without him getting into trouble,' she declared. 'I always said that girls would be the death of him one of these days.'

There was general laughter. Tongues were loosened as more explanations were sought and given. After that the conversation continued on a more superficial level with talk of holiday experiences and so forth.

It was certainly no occasion for the discussion of family matters. All the same, Christina was aware of powerful undercurrents and unspoken thoughts as people sized each other up. She caught Piers quietly observing her relatives, and her aunt eyeing her husband when he chatted flirtatiously with Donna and herself. Her uncle Henry might well be carried away by a pretty face, she discovered, and her aunt Beth was patently disapproving. It turned out to be an agreeable dinner party, however. The ice had been broken and Christina was happy to leave talk of more intimate things until she visited Herne Bay.

At the end of the evening it was Henry who offered the hospitality. With his arm affectionately around her, he kissed her heartily. 'Now just you remember, Christina, our home is your home. You must come whenever you like. Mustn't she, Beth?'

'Yes, of course,' his wife said, between a bout of

coughing, 'so long as she takes us as she finds us. I lost my cleaning lady before we went away and I've yet to find another.'

'I'll be coming to see you, not the house,' Christina returned, smiling. 'Of course I'd ring first, to see if it was convenient——'

'You're so like your mother when you smile like that,' Henry interrupted, giving her a gentle squeeze. 'Isn't she, Beth?'

'Yes, but don't keep on about it,' his wife said tetchily, her cough increasingly troublesome.

'Don't you have an atomiser to help with your asthma?' Christina asked, looking concerned.

'I do, but I didn't bring it with me. I'll be all right once I'm in the fresh air.' Aunt Beth tugged her husband's sleeve. 'Come on, Henry, it's time we went.'

'Tell you what,' Henry said, still lingering. 'Why don't the four of you come for dinner, say next weekend?'

Christina felt embarrassed. She gave Piers a sideways glance. It seemed to have been taken for granted that there was something between her and the registrar. 'Well—um——' she hesitated '—next weekend I'm working. I don't know about the others.'

'Oh, yes, I was forgetting you lot don't work nine-to-five,' her uncle returned. 'You'll just have to sort something out between you and let us know.'

It had started to rain, and in the car park there were hurried kisses and handshakes in parting before the couples set off, all in different directions, for their homes. For the first few minutes Christina was silent, sitting alongside the equally silent doctor. Not knowing quite where to start, she began, 'Piers, I must apologise that you got let in for—all of this tonight.'

'Let in for all what?' he asked mildly.

'Oh, my domestic affairs, and getting treated as—um—being asked to join a family get-together, and so on. You don't have to come, you know. I'll explain...'

Piers drew to a halt as the traffic-lights flashed red. He turned to face her. 'If there's any explaining to be done, I can do it myself, Miss Linden. Do I gather that you'd rather I didn't accept the invitation?'

With his face in shadow she couldn't manage to read his expression, but he wasn't smiling. 'I don't care whether you do or not,' she declared with a shrug. 'I just didn't want you to think—I mean, you know it had nothing at all to do with me that you were asked to come tonight. You do believe that I knew nothing about it, don't you?'

He re-started the car when the traffic-lights changed to green. 'Yes, I believe you.'

'Fine,' she breathed.

'And don't you try to do me out of a decent family nosh-up. Besides, this saga could run and run. With my stepsister being one of the key players, I am an interested party, aren't I?'

Christina couldn't help but giggle. 'I thought you didn't want to get involved in her affairs?'

'Ah! Didn't want and duty bound are two very different things, and the choice isn't always easy.'

She felt less awkward now, finding him in a whimsical frame of mind. This was the man she was beginning to know—a man of principle, but also conscious of his own weaknesses. 'Actually, it was sweet of Donna to suggest you partner me. And it did help. It wasn't a bad evening really, was it?' She glanced wistfully at his attractive profile.

'Not bad at all,' he replied. 'Fascinating.'

At a loss to know whether he really meant it, she studied the glistening road ahead as they approached the hospital and hoped he didn't actually believe it had been a wasted evening. Impulsively she blurted out, 'If you could wait a moment when we get to the hostel I do have something for you, but it's in my room.'

'Even more fascinating,' he joked, turning in through the main entrance. 'What is it?'

'The ward plan I've drawn up.'

'You've done it?'

'Yes, I finished it a couple of days ago but I hadn't seen you—not to talk to—and there are a couple of things which need explaining.'

He drove carefully past the main group of hospital buildings towards the quiet road leading to the nurses' quarters. 'I must confess to being pleasantly surprised,' he said.

'I don't see why. I told you I meant it. Perhaps it will make this evening not such a total waste of your time after all.'

He drew to a halt outside the hostel. 'I didn't say it was a waste of time, did I? Off you go, then. I'll wait here.'

She slipped out of the car, ran through the drizzle and up to her room, and returned with her plan in a foolscap envelope.

Piers leaned across to push open the passenger door. 'You'd better hop in again,' he said. She did as he asked and started to take the paper out of the envelope. 'Look, we can hardly discuss this thing properly here, can we?' he went on.

'No, I suppose not. There is our communal sitting-room, or would you rather wait till. . .?'

'How would you feel about coming back to my place? It's not far—and you can talk me through it in comfort.'

Christina was taken by surprise; her pulse began to race. She checked her wristwatch, to give herself time to think.

'Come on, it's only ten-thirty. Not past your bedtime yet, surely,' he quipped.

Her laugher was a little uncertain. 'No, I am on a late tomorrow.'

'Right, then—and I'll throw in coffee as well. Will Mason lives in one of the flats near me. If he's around we could ask him to join us and give his opinion. OK by you?'

She nodded. He reversed the car and drove back the way they had come.

'So how did you feel about this first meeting with the family?' he asked cheerfully.

'Great!' she said, without much conviction.

'Your uncle Henry was certainly very welcoming.'

'I don't think Aunt Beth was feeling too well, which is probably why she was subdued.'

'Hmm,' Piers murmured.

'What does that mean? You didn't like her?' Christina asked defensively.

'I've no opinion one way or the other. But I did wonder, from the fuss your uncle made of you, whether he was as attentive to your mother before they left the country. Could that have been the trouble between the sisters?'

Similar thoughts had strayed across Christina's subconscious. The idea seemed possible, but she refused to admit it. She didn't want anything to spoil the atmosphere with her new-found family. 'Oh, that's rather fanciful,' she scoffed. 'Anyway, it's a long time ago now. No point in resurrecting the past.'

'True! Forget it. I knew you were a sensible girl.'

A fifteen-minute drive brought them to the wooded grounds of a block of luxury flats. Lights flooded out from the impressive glassed-in vestibule, with further security doors leading to lifts and individual apartments. Piers put his key into the door of one of the ground-floor flats. She followed him into a very untidy living-room, well-furnished but cluttered. He closed the russet velour curtains over the large, rain-spattered window, swept a pile of newspapers off a deep-cushioned settee and motioned her to sit down.

'Take off your jacket. I'll give Will a ring before I make coffee.' He picked up the telephone on his leather-topped desk and dialled, but after a few moments he replaced the receiver. 'Not there; pity. So it's just you and me.' Sorting through a pile of things, he picked out a plastic bag with a familiar bookseller's imprint and passed it to her. 'There you are, something for you. I shan't be a moment.'

Inside the bag she found a slim volume with a colourful cover, entitled *Wild Flowers of the British Isles*.

'Is this for me?' she asked, holding it up with a delighted smile, when he came back with two steaming mugs of coffee.

'I happened to see it and thought you might like it,' he said casually. 'I looked up that blue flower you pointed out by the roadside the other day. Think it's called chicory—the stuff they sometimes put with coffee to make it stronger.'

'Oh! You have been busy,' she said. 'Have I started you on a new interest?'

He sat down beside her on the settee. 'I'll pass on that. Now, what about this wonderful ward plan of yours?'

She took it out of the envelope and spread it out on the coffee-table. 'It's very basic, all quite straightforward really. Five six-bedded bays, divided by curtains. Luckily the bathrooms, sluice and other amenities are all on the right-hand side, so there are no real structural problems. The maintenance department ought to be able to fix up the overhead rails, and I'm sure the electricians shouldn't have too much difficulty in fixing up the lighting and radio points. Of course it would need a more professional plan than this. But it's the only paper I had. It is to scale. I measured the beds and the space between them.'

He had been quiet all the while she had been speaking. Now she looked at him and said, 'Well, what do you think? It looks possible, doesn't it, and wouldn't cost the earth?'

Passing a hand over his dark jaw, Piers said, 'Hmm! Quite honestly I'd never given it any real thought until this moment. But it does seem worth consideration, Christina. Well done! I think it would be best to get a draughtsman to draw up a more sizeable blueprint to submit to the committee. That's something I could get my father to do for us. He's the chairman of Conrad Constructions. He's got a whole army of professionals at his disposal.'

Christina was thrilled that he wasn't dismissing the whole idea out of hand. 'So you think it might work?' she asked eagerly.

'Drink your coffee,' he replied, exasperatingly non-committal. 'I'm prepared to put it to the experts and see what happens.'

'And they'll take forever thinking about it.' She groaned. 'I know the way these committees work.'

'Well, there's still the question of having to close the ward while it's done—although it may be due for redecoration anyway.' Piers chuckled. 'Patience, my sweet. Rome wasn't built in a day. But if and when the idea takes off don't be surprised if someone else gets the credit for what you thought of,' he warned her. 'That's life.'

'Who cares who gets the credit, so long as it makes the patients more comfortable?' Christina replied.

He leaned back against the cushions, pushing his hands through his dark hair, giving her a roguish glance. 'And are you also doing your bit to provide the funds—helping to make up our knock-out team?'

'No,' she said. 'They had enough without me.'

'Did they? Well, you can't get off scot-free, young

woman. I need a partner for the treasure hunt. How about joining me?'

She laughed softly, never mind her stomach turning a somersault. 'Do I have any option?'

'No. You're the only girl I feel free to ask. At least I can be sure you won't go reading romantic overtones into it.'

Christina drew a steadying breath and chewed her lip for a moment. 'Rest assured, there's absolutely no danger of my doing that,' she said, smiling.

She jumped up and began putting on her jacket. 'Come on, hadn't you better take me home?'

It was midnight by the time he returned her to the nurses' hostel. They had both been unusually quiet on the journey, the rain making driving hazardous. Pulling up outside, Piers growled, 'Isn't it time you got out of this dump, if you intend to stay?'

'I'm thinking about it,' she said. 'Justin promised he'd look out for something for me, but I guess he's been a bit tied up lately.'

He made a wry face. 'Now there's an understatement for you. Fortunately his romance does seem to be a two-way thing. Let's hope his mother doesn't mind.'

She released her seatbelt and prepared to get out of the car.

'Don't forget this.' He passed her the book on wild flowers which she had put on the dashboard.

'Oh, no. Thank you very much. Bye.' She turned to him with an engaging smile. After the oddly intimate evening they had spent together it didn't seem right somehow just to slip out of the car and go. She wanted very much to kiss him—but that was quite definitely out of the question. And Piers' attitude was far from inviting, sitting there gripping the wheel as though he couldn't wait to be gone.

Running through the rain, Christina let herself into the building and climbed the stairs to her room. She felt as if she had lived through a lifetime since the evening began. Throwing off her damp clothes, she put on her comfortable towelling robe, as if the familiar action would wipe out disturbing memories of the registrar, but of course it couldn't.

While she was brushing her teeth as she prepared for bed, her mind went racing back to her meeting with her aunt and uncle—reminding her of Piers' speculation that there might have been jealousy between Beth and Christina's mother. And that prompted all sorts of other questions she had no wish to analyse.

As for Piers himself, it was obvious that there was some kind of chemistry between the pair of them, whether he was prepared to admit it or not. There was no doubt he was afraid of love. The trouble was Christina found that her feelings for him were deepening by the minute. He had only to appear and her heart sang, but if he guessed as much he would run a mile. At least while she played it cool she could keep his friendship. That was better than nothing, she supposed. Or would it in the end prove to be too hard to handle?

CHAPTER SEVEN

THE relentless rain of the past few days had cast gloom over prospects for the hospital's centenary celebrations. Now, at last, the clouds had lifted, the sky was blue and the countryside looked newly washed and revitalised. Christina and Judy, making their way to the canteen for a light lunch before starting work, had a spring in their step.

'Thank goodness it's cleared up at last,' Judy said, avoiding a puddle. 'Will has asked me to go on the car treasure hunt with him. It wouldn't have been much fun in the rain.'

'No-o,' Christina returned thoughtfully. 'Piers asked me to be his partner for that, but I don't know much about it yet. Do you?'

'Yes, I've been on one of these things before,' Judy chatted. 'There'll be a sheet of clues, and a map with reference points. There's no time limit as a rule, but all entries have to be in by a certain date. It's good fun. Depending on who you're with, of course. Being with Will, I'm really looking forward to this one, although I know he hasn't got a serious thought in his head.' Pausing, she gave Christina an enquiring glance. 'You say you're going with Piers—should I read anything into that?'

'Good heavens, no!' Christina hooted, handing her friend a tray as they queued at the canteen counter for their lunch. 'What with my cousin Justin dating Piers' stepsister, we seem almost like family. I think he feels that makes me safe territory.'

Judy chuckled. 'Believe that and you'll believe anything.'

'It's true! He as good as told me so.'

'Oh, yeah! Why is he entering the treasure hunt, then, if not for the pleasure of your company?'

'For the same reason as you and Will, of course.' Christina smiled wryly. 'For the hell of it, and to do his bit towards our ward effort.'

'Ah! But we all know Will's a rolling stone. Piers isn't like that,' Judy insisted, shaking her dark head and looking wise.

They carried their food to a table. Christina had happened to catch sight of Donna, sitting with some of her friends in a far corner. She made no comment although privately she wondered where the girl was working. Her curiosity was soon to be satisfied, however, when Donna, on finishing her meal, came bounding across to talk.

'Hi!' she said brightly. 'Do excuse me butting in.' Smiling first at Judy, she turned to Christina. 'I believe I'm going to be working with you. Aren't you on ward nine?'

Christina nodded. 'Yes, I am.'

'Oh, terrific. It'll be great having someone I know there.' Donna patted her white-uniformed chest in a gesture of relief. She lifted back her flowing brown hair. 'I'm just about to go and put up my locks or I'll have the sister on my back, won't I? What's she like?'

'Helen Yates? She's fine. In fact, so are the rest of the staff on there.' Christina smiled encouragingly at the girl. 'You'll be OK.'

Donna gave a heartfelt sigh. 'I dread my first days on a new ward, until I get used to it. And this allocation is going to be ten times worse with Piers hovering in the background as the medical reg. How's he to work with?'

'He's tolerable,' Christina grinned. 'Anyway, I don't suppose you'll have that much to do with him.' She paused, watching Donna anxiously nibbling her thumbnail. 'Are you feeling all right? You look a bit pale.'

'Actually I was sick this morning,' the girl admitted with a light laugh. 'It was either something I ate or panic. The thought of all those strange faces looking at you from a row of beds—it scares me to death.'

Christina smiled sympathetically. 'You only have to be nice to them and you'll have friends for life. Cheer up—you'll soon settle in.'

'Oh, thanks, Christina. I do hope so.' Donna went on her way to fix her hair, looking a little happier.

'Remember what it was like when you were a beginner?' Judy smiled, watching her go.

'Do I ever! Anyway, she'll be fine with Helen and Patrick, so long as she pulls her weight. *My* first sister was an absolute dragon,' Christina recalled. 'But she knew how to run a ward.'

The two senior nurses went their separate ways. When Christina reached the ward she found that Donna had already arrived and was in the office, her plentiful hair neatly braided in place.

'Everyone here?' Helen enquired briskly. 'Right—this is Donna,' she told the others. 'She's going to be with us for a while, in place of Rachel. She's here to learn, so help her as much as possible. Karen, you can be her mentor for this afternoon.' After giving her report, the sister then went off to her own lunch.

'Well, come on, then, Donna,' Karen said in a bored tone of voice, 'I'd better show you where everything is first of all. Then there's a care plan to write out for that new patient, Mr West.'

Going off to see to her own patients, Christina thought that Helen might have made a happier choice than to leave Donna in Karen's tender care. But she was also quite glad not to have been landed with the job herself. Of course she would willingly help Donna whenever necessary, but she had a feeling it would be best not to get too personally involved with the girl.

'Hello, Lucy,' Christina greeted her thyrotoxic patient brightly. 'How are you today? You saw the neurologist this morning, didn't you?'

Lucy had a welcoming smile for her and was much more relaxed than when admitted just under a week ago. 'Yes, he was very reassuring,' she volunteered. 'He said this weakness in my arms and legs is all down to my over-active thyroid, and it should improve after the operation.'

'That's great. So, you might be able to go home at the weekend, all being well. They'll probably put you on a course of Lugol's iodine before you come back for the operation. That's the usual course of action.' Christina set about checking her patient's vital signs.

'I feel so much better, after the medicine I've been getting here, I almost wonder if the operation's going to be necessary,' Lucy said.

Christina nodded her head positively. 'Oh, yes, the drugs are highly effective, but you can't stay on those forever. Is it the scar round your neck you're worried about? There's no need—that will scarcely be visible in time. And you'll get rid of the swelling, and your eyes will be less staring,' she pointed out encouragingly. 'The surgeon explained everything to you, I expect. Didn't he?'

'Well, not really,' Lucy said, 'but Dr Conrad came back later to make sure I'd understood. He was with me for about twenty minutes. He's so nice, isn't he?'

'Yes, he makes time for people,' Christina agreed, smiling. 'Well, your obs are pretty good now. I'll go and get your tablets.'

With Helen not yet back from lunch, Christina went in search of Karen for the drugs-trolley keys and found her in the ward kitchen having a mug of tea.

'Oh, I was going to do the drugs myself in a minute, but you might as well carry on, then,' she said. 'And take that new girl with you. That'll keep her occupied until I've got time to get down to George West's care plan with her. She went to the sluice to get someone a bottle. That was over ten minutes ago. Some people!' Karen denounced scathingly.

Christina grinned. 'Give her a break. You know what it's like when you're new.'

The staff nurse rolled her eyes and half smiled. 'It's so long ago I've forgotten. Want a cuppa? There's one in the pot.'

'Not now, thanks. I'd better get on or we'll have visitors here.'

'OK. Leave the injections. I'll see to those myself,' Karen said.

Going to the sluice-room, Christina found Donna there, painstakingly washing her hands. 'Hi!' the girl said, glancing up with an anxious smile. 'You take one person a bottle and they all want one. Karen will be wondering what I'm up to.'

'Not to worry,' Christina said, 'Karen's busy with something else at the moment. Like to come and help me with the drugs?'

'Great! If you're sure that it's all right with Karen. Only I wouldn't like to get on the wrong side of her,' Donna murmured.

'Look, don't let anyone intimidate you,' Christina advised. 'If you're doing your best, you can't do more. Karen's not bad really; she's just got a rather unfortunate manner.'

Donna laughed. 'That's one way of putting it.'

'When you're ready, then.' With a private smile Christina went to collect the drugs trolley.

During the round she gave Donna a brief rundown of the patients and the reason for any particular medication, stressing the importance of checking the patient's wristband against the medication chart, to avoid error.

'Oh, I do know that. I'm not a complete wally,' Donna laughed.

'No offence,' Christina returned mildly, 'only we can't afford to make mistakes.'

Coming to Mr Chalice, now bright of eye and sitting alongside his bed in a Paisley silk dressing-gown, Christina gave him a wide smile. 'My word, you look like a new man, Mr Chalice,' she said. 'Donna, you would never have recognised him if you'd seen him when he first came to us.'

The patient chuckled. 'I don't remember much about those days myself, but my wife thinks you're all miracle workers here.'

Christina dispensed his tablets. Donna checked his wristband, poured him a drink and waited while he swallowed.

'Thank you, lassie,' he said. 'We haven't met before, have we?'

'No, I've only just joined the miracle workers.' Donna gave the pensioner a cheeky grin.

He jerked a thumb towards Christina. 'You take a leaf out of her book and you won't go far wrong. Well, it seems I'll be leaving you soon, eh, Nurse? They want to get my plumbing sorted out, once they've done a few more tests.' He sounded a little apprehensive. 'It's the old prostate business...'

'Yes, don't worry about it, Mr Chalice. It's a fairly straightforward operation these days,' Christina reassured him. 'No external wound to heal. All being well you should be up and about again within a week or so.'

He nodded. 'So I was given to understand. Amazing that, isn't it?'

The nurses moved on and finished their round.

'Thanks, Christina,' Donna said. 'What shall I do now? Better go and ask Karen, I suppose.' She sighed wistfully, gazing out of a sunny window. 'I can think of better ways of spending a lovely afternoon like this. Justin was going to Sandwich today.'

'Well, you'll have your days off before long.' Christina was only half listening as she closed and locked the drugs trolley. 'Justin's time seems to be pretty much his own,' she remarked, hesitating. 'You two are seeing quite a lot of each other, aren't you?'

'Oh, yes, as much as we can.' Donna's face was radiant. 'It's crazy, I know,' she said, 'but just seeing him makes my world light up.'

Christina smiled and went about her own work. She knew how Donna felt. It was a similar effect that Piers had on her. But whereas Donna was at liberty to give full range to her emotions, Christina's feelings had to be kept strictly under wraps.

Later that afternoon, on the way to her tea-break, Christina paused to study the Society of Friends noticeboard and saw that map references and clues for the treasure hunt would be obtainable as from Friday at the Friends shop. The completed questionnaires were to be handed in a week later. Although Piers had not spoken again to her about it, she supposed they were still on as a team.

Walking along daydreaming, envious of Donna's good fortune and wishing her own feelings for the registrar were not so tumultuous, she rounded a corner and cannoned into the man himself. Blushing wildly, as though he could read her thoughts, she laughed and said, 'Oh! It's you.'

'On your own private cloud, as usual, were you?' Piers returned. 'Where are you off to?' His perceptive hazel eyes smiling down at her were enquiring.

'Just going for my tea,' she said.

'Are you meeting someone, or could we have tea together? We need to talk, don't we?'

She stiffened her guard against the seductive power of his enthralling voice. 'You mean about the treasure hunt? No, I'm not meeting anyone.'

'Good!' He strolled along beside her, talking amiably. 'I hear you're to have the pleasure of working with my little stepsister for a time.'

'Yes, she's on duty with me this afternoon, actually.'

'How's she shaping?'

'She's finding her feet.' Christina glanced up at him and took a long breath before going on. 'I'd really rather you didn't ask me about Donna in that respect. You should ask Helen if you want to know how she's doing.'

Piers laughed softly. 'Yes, I realise that was out of order. Anyway, it wasn't a serious enquiry.'

In the cafeteria they collected tea and buttered buns and sat at a side-table for two. 'What day will you have free next week?' he wanted to know.

'Wednesday and Thursday. The people taking part in the knock-out competition had to be given precedence for the weekend,' she told him.

He reached for a notebook in the pocket of his white coat and turned a few pages. 'Right—I can be available on Wednesday, if that suits you?'

'Fine!' she agreed. 'What about picking up the entry forms—shall I do that or will you?'

He thought for a moment, stirring his tea. 'I will. It'll give me a chance to plot a route. I'll let you know later what time we need to start.'

Their eyes met across the table and they smiled at each other. 'I'm looking forward to it,' she said, having to lower her gaze from his. 'I'll be able to see a bit more of the countryside.'

'This isn't supposed to be a pleasure jaunt, you know. The object is to earn some points towards getting your ward project off the ground,' he replied, curbing a grin. 'Maybe I'll let you stargaze from time to time, though. Now if you'll excuse me, Christina, I should really be somewhere else.' Hastily he finished his tea, bade her a brief goodbye and left.

Christina finished her own tea, outwardly calm although her inner feelings were far from tranquil. She was aware that a few curious glances from other members of staff had drifted their way, so it was important to appear detached and not to excite gossip. That was what Piers would wish, she knew. But it wasn't easy when inside her heart was racing. In fact, although she couldn't help but be thrilled at the prospect of her outing with Piers, there was that other sensible part of her which advised caution. To be in his company for as long as the treasure hunt took, that would be utter bliss. Sadly, however, it was a road leading nowhere.

The weekend passed uneventfully, and it wasn't until Tuesday night as she was leaving the ward that Piers came to find her.

'Just the girl I was looking for,' he announced cheerfully, falling into step beside her as she made towards the lift. 'It was tomorrow we agreed for this safari, wasn't it?'

'Yes, I was beginning to wonder if you'd forgotten,' she said levelly.

'Dear me, no! I had it filed away in my brain, under "Matters of Great Importance",' he joked. 'I was speaking to someone who's already done it. There's a good bit of ground to cover, apparently, and there's no knowing how long it'll take us to solve these clues. It depends on how bright you're feeling.'

'And you!' she answered back.

'Oh, I'm content to be the driver in this partnership. You can be the brains,' he teased. 'I'll pick you up at ten—that all right?'.

'Mmm, fine,' she agreed.

'OK. See you in the morning. Goodnight, Christina.' And he retraced his steps back towards the ward.

Waking very early the following morning, she threw back the curtains on a bright, promising day. Nothing but the white trail of a distant aircraft broke the halcyon blue of the sky, and a breath of the countryside drifted in on the light morning breeze. Banishing negative thoughts, Christina hugged herself with pleasure at the prospect of the day ahead. She stood for a moment enjoying the pleasant sound of birdsong from the nearby trees, then gathered up her toilet bag and towels and made for the bathroom.

Going through the motions of everyday living seemed a tedious chore and every minute an hour when she couldn't wait for the time to fly until she could be with Piers. Sternly she reminded herself to stop being ridiculous, towelling dry her honeyed hair with more than necessary vigour. Piers saw her as nothing more than an acceptable working companion, and she had better believe it. All the same, it was impossible to subdue the exhilaration that welled inside her.

Deliberately dressing for comfort rather than effect, she slipped into a pair of white jeans and a simple apricot T-shirt, brushing her hair loose about her shoulders. Sensible white trainers on her feet, in case there should be any rough country to cover, a lightweight jacket to sling in the back of the car, and she was ready and waiting when Piers drew up outside the hostel a few minutes after ten.

Also casually dressed, in black jeans and a creamy sweatshirt, he greeted her with an appreciative smile as he came round to open the passenger door of the white BMW.

'You're looking daisy-fresh,' he said, his eyes running over her slender frame. 'Hope that means you've got all your wits about you.'

She laughed. 'I'll do my best. You did pick up the entry forms?'

'Of course. They're there, on your seat. I've spent

a little while working out a route of sorts.'

She picked up the photocopied papers as she entered the car. He closed the door after her and went round to his own side. Studying the map, and the way he had marked it, she saw that he had worked out a kind of circular tour, taking in a number of villages she had heard of but not yet visited. There were reference numbers all along the route, tying in with the twelve clues listed on a separate sheet.

'I suppose you've been to most of these places before,' she remarked, stealing a glance at his fascinating profile while he adjusted the side-mirror before setting off.

'Some of them.' He paused, turning to look at her. 'I've also got a good gazetteer, remember?'

She smiled, casting her mind back and remembering very well. 'Yes, that trip to Herne Bay seems a long time ago now.'

'Has anything more been said about the suggested family get-together?' Piers asked as they drove away.

'No, I haven't been in touch again since,' Christina admitted. 'Thought I'd leave it to Justin to sort out. It'll have to be after the centenary weekend now, I expect, with everyone being busy,' she added evasively.

He laughed aloud. 'Christina! I had you down as a doer, not a wimp. What are you scared of?'

'Nothing—and everything.' She gave a rueful grin. 'I thought—you can't just barge into people's lives after eighteen years' absence and expect to be accepted, just like that. They know I'm here. I don't want to push my luck. Anyway, let's forget that for now and get down to business.' She returned her attention to the map. 'Which way are we heading?'

The corners of his mouth twitched ironically, but he bowed to her wishes. 'We'll start at Chartham, then go on to Chilham, et cetera. I've arrowed the way. You can tie up the clues.'

As they travelled down leafy country lanes to their first village stop, Christina studied the cryptic clues, smiling as she read them. 'Someone's gone to a lot of trouble dreaming up this lot,' she said. 'At Chartham we have to find out the name of the minister of the fourteenth-century church there.'

'Well, that doesn't sound too challenging,' Piers returned. 'There's bound to be a noticeboard.'

In a short while they had reached their destination, and the historic old church by the large village green was easy enough to find. Piers drew to a halt near by. 'Out you get, then,' he said. 'Expect you'll find the required information over there somewhere.'

She threw him a patient smile, tugged an imaginary forelock, and said, 'Yes, sir!' Crossing to the impressive building, she stood for a moment admiring its noble lines and fine tower. The name she needed was on the board, as Piers had supposed, and after carefully making a note of it she returned, somewhat reluctantly, to the car.

'OK?' he asked.

'Yes, fine. That's our first two points in the bag.'

He grinned. 'It won't be much of a contest if they're all as easy as that, will it?'

'Oh, that's just for starters.' Christina busied herself writing the answer on the form. 'How are you on anagrams? We've got one of those to solve presently.'

'As I said, the brains is your department, milady.'

She glanced back at the grand old place of worship, a testament to times past. 'I would love to have a look inside that church,' she said, 'but I suppose we don't really have the time today.'

'Afraid not.' Piers drove on. 'We ought to get to Chilham before all the tourists arrive. It's a kind of showplace—the sort they put on calendars. What are we looking for there?'

Christina took her admiring eyes from the wild sweep of the countryside where a ribbon of sparkling water found its way through the foothills. She consulted the sheet of clues. 'We have to find out...why this large dog is no threat to anyone,' she read.

For a moment Piers made no reply, then he smiled. 'Chained up—or a model dog somewhere,' he said.

'I thought you'd decided I was to be the brains of this outfit?' Christina challenged.

'You can solve the anagram. I don't mind helping with the easy ones,' he cracked.

Nearing Chilham, they parked outside the village centre and climbed the steep lane to the main square. On reaching it Christina paused, looking about her in delight. As Piers had said, it presented a charming picture. Many of the well-preserved black and white Tudor houses on either side of the square were decorated with flower-filled hanging baskets. A square-towered grey Norman church sat at the far end, while at the other the scenic parkland of a stately home completed the view.

'Well, what do you think of it?' Piers asked, eyeing her complacently.

'Wow! It's certainly worth seeing.' Christina's eyes shone. 'Everything here must be centuries old.'

'Yes, it's seen a fair bit of history in the making,' he returned with a quiet smile. 'We must plan a proper sightseeing tour for you one of these days. Right now, though, we're supposed to be looking for a dog of some kind. So come on...'

Other streets led out from the central square, but their clue was to be found somewhere in the middle. They mingled with other people wandering around the miscellany of shops and presently tracked down what they both agreed must be their quarry—a life-sized model of a golden Labrador tethered outside a teashop, seeking donations for Guide Dogs for the Blind.

Patting the model on the head, Piers placed a contribution in the slot provided. 'We had a dog similar to this while I was growing up,' he recalled. 'Great character, he was.'

'Lucky you. I never had a pet,' she admitted. 'Somehow it was never convenient.'

By this time it was midday. Piers led her towards the local historic pub, also bright with hanging baskets. 'Let's get something to eat before we tackle the next thing on the agenda. My stomach's rumbling—I only had coffee for breakfast. How about you?'

'Yes, sounds like a good idea,' Christina agreed, although, being with Piers, food was the last thing on her mind. 'We mustn't waste time, though,' she reminded him. 'There's still an awful lot to do.'

'An army marches on its stomach, remember,' he returned.

'If you say so.' She laughed, 'And when were you in the army?'

'I haven't been, not that kind of army anyway. But I did a spell of VSO in East Africa, when it was important to keep oneself fit,' he explained.

They lunched lightly on chicken and crisp salad sandwiches, washed down with ice-cold cider and accompanied by lively repartee. They continued their journey in mutual enjoyment, coming to know each other even better as the day progressed.

On reaching the pleasant old market town of Wye, an inn called The New Flying Horse seemed the appropriate answer to the question 'Is this a descendant of Pegasus?' At a country park near by they were able to work out their anagram as being the sign on a farm gate which read 'Keep Dogs on Lead'.

For Christina it was a tour of enchantment. Their

search led them to hamlets and villages in out-of-the-way places, where occasional pheasants strutted recklessly along hedgerows in narrow lanes. She had never seen so many remote and remarkable old churches. Every village seemed to have one, as well as an attractive old inn or two. They passed orchards on the hillsides and lakes in the valleys, grand mansions, and quaint thatched cottages. And it was all the more thrilling for her because of this captivating man at her side.

'Well, that should be twenty-four Brownie points for us,' Piers said blithely, watching her fold the paper and tuck it away in her shoulder-bag. They were sitting on a riverside bank, having just identified the name of the person who had donated the seat, the answer to their last clue. 'I've really enjoyed this. I hope you have.'

'Very much,' she replied. 'I'd like to do it all again and spend more time everywhere.'

He put his arm about her shoulders and gave her a hug. 'We must see what we can do about that. Now, how about this fair on Saturday—will you be able to get there?'

She shook her head. 'Working until nine.'

'Tough! But at least that should free you for the following weekend and the ball,' he said. 'It should be a good show.'

She smiled wanly, sad that this was the end of their day together. Their friendship had deepened, but it was no more than that. She felt like taking him by the lapels and yelling at him, I love you, *I love you. Please* love me too! But that was the last thing she must do. If anything was to happen between them, he had to start it himself. She sighed deeply.

Piers put a hand under her chin and turned her face to look at him. 'Why the big sigh?' he asked. 'What are you worried about?'

Laughing, she shook her head free. 'Nothing. It was just one of those moments.'

He hesitated, as though weighing up pros and cons, then brushed her lips with his own. 'I'm glad you came to North Downs. Shall I take you to dinner tonight?'

Christina smoothed back her hair with both hands, listening to a small inner voice which whispered, Don't sound too ecstatic! 'Yes, that would be nice,' she replied smoothly.

He gave a one-sided grin. 'Do I detect a certain lack of enthusiasm?'

'No, it's not that,' she hastened to say. 'I'm just in need of a wash and change, that's all.'

He checked his wristwatch. 'It's five o'clock now. I'll drop you back at your place and pick you up again at, say, seven. All right?'

'Yes, fine.'

Their route home was via winding country lanes. Piers had put on a cassette of pleasant background music. Both of them were quiet as the powerful car rolled along the narrow byways. Sometimes they passed undulating grassy slopes dotted with sheep, or stands of woodland, or a forest of hop-poles. They came to a lane edged by banks of brambles and briars and tall weeds, and to the right a wide ditch ran full after the recent rains. Nothing passed them coming from the opposite direction, although there was mud on the road where a tractor had turned down a rough farm track. Slowing the car to round a curve, Piers barely had time to pick up speed before they passed a smart green Rover lying on its side in the ditch among the vegetation.

Christina looked back. 'Oh, dear!' she exclaimed. 'Someone had a nasty accident.'

Piers had driven by, but now he braked and reversed. 'Not much moving on this road. I ought to check that there's no one still inside. You stay put.'

Pulling into a passing-place, he leapt out and strode the ten yards back to investigate.

Leaning across to his side of the car, Christina watched him out of the open window. She saw him step up on to the bank and, with some difficulty, peer inside the wreck. She saw his expression change to one of disbelief and concern as he wrenched open the passenger door and clambered up.

Her heart beating wildly, Christina ran back to join him. 'I'm here,' she called out. 'Anything I can do?'

Piers climbed down from his vantage point. 'There's a guy in there,' he told her. 'He's unconscious, but I found a radial pulse. Can't get to him properly, though. Christina, we need help quickly. There's water seeping into the car, and we can't move him. Get my mobile phone. It's in the door pocket.'

Christina flew back to the doctor's car to do as he asked. When she returned, he told her in significant tones, 'We know this man—it's Colin Rhodes!'

CHAPTER EIGHT

CHRISTINA discovered that they were not far away from the city, despite the seeming isolation of their position. With Piers able to give the emergency services the exact location of the accident, the ambulance could be expected within fifteen minutes.

'Who is Colin Rhodes?' she asked in a low voice when he had finished telephoning.

'He's on the business management committee of the hospital.'

'Oh!' Her eyes widened.

Piers climbed back into the car beside the casualty. Holding the man's hand, he spoke to him by name, looking for signs of returning consciousness. 'I don't think he could have been here long,' he told Christina. 'I had to switch off the engine.'

'Poor guy. How badly hurt is he—can you say?' Christina pulled herself up into the back of the car and leaned across to look. Her heart filled with compassion at the sight of the prostrate victim. His fleshy face was bruised and cut from the shattered windscreen. Lank dark hair was plastered across his clammy forehead. His right arm seemed at a curious angle.

'His pupils are equal and reacting—pulse regular. Thank goodness he was wearing his seatbelt. That's possibly saved any rib damage,' Piers went on. 'There's no external bleeding as far as I can see, but he may have a dislocated shoulder there.' As the doctor was speaking the casualty made a low moaning sound and his eyelids fluttered. 'All right, old chap, don't try to move,' Piers said in a soothing voice. 'You've had an accident in your car. There's an ambulance on its way.'

'Oh, God!' the man mumbled, followed by incoherent words they could scarcely make out.

Christina smoothed away the dark hair from a cut on his eyebrow. 'Help will soon be here, Mr Rhodes,' she said gently.

'P-papers—papers,' he gabbled. 'Mustn't lose—my papers. . .'

Looking around, she saw that there was a briefcase on the back seat. 'It's all right, Colin,' she reassured him. 'We know who you are and we'll take care of your things. This is Dr Conrad here with you—from the hospital. . .'

The ambulance siren heralded its approach. Piers jumped down to greet the paramedics and give them what details he could. 'It's not going to be easy to get him out of there,' he said. 'He's quite a heavyweight.'

After the fitting of a surgical collar, it needed all available hands to free Mr Rhodes from his wrecked car. At last, successfully transferred to the stretcher, his condition was easier to assess. Miraculously, apart from the dislocated shoulder which was giving him considerable pain, he seemed to have escaped other serious injury. The blow to his head which had knocked him out had left him dazed and confused, but the extent of that could only be determined by X-ray.

'Let's give him some pethidine to make him more comfortable,' Piers decided, 'and a Haemacell line would be a good idea, if you have one.'

'We certainly do,' the young paramedic confirmed. They set about putting up the drip.

In spite of his physical distress, Mr Rhodes was still rambling on about the contents of his car and what was to happen to it. Christina once again told him in a comforting voice that all would be taken care of.

The narrow lane had now become blocked in both directions. There were police cars and a sudden build-up of other traffic, but at last the patient was loaded into the ambulance and a way cleared for its departure.

'You knew the casualty, did you, sir?' a policeman queried, talking to Piers afterwards and preparing to take a statement.

'Yes—professionally speaking, that is. We both work at North Downs Hospital. I can't tell you how the accident occurred. We just saw the car lying in the ditch and decided to investigate. He was unconscious when we found him.'

After supplying what other information he could, Piers agreed to take charge of Mr Rhodes' personal property, so that a breakdown lorry could remove the wreckage from the highway.

In due course, Christina and Piers were able to continue their journey home.

'I'm afraid that's our evening meal washed out for tonight, Christina,' Piers said regretfully. 'I'll have to go over to Casualty and see how our friend is faring.'

'Yes, of course,' she said. 'He's going to be all right, though, isn't he?'

'Should think so, although I know nothing about his physical condition prior to the accident.' The registrar paused for a moment. 'As a matter of fact,' he went on, 'I actually had a meeting with him only a few days ago. He's the person I submitted your ward plan to.'

Christina's eyes widened yet again. 'Really? What was his reaction?'

'Non-committal at the time, but that didn't surprise me. However, it *might* go in your favour that we came to his assistance today,' he added with a slight smile.

'I'd never even seen him before,' Christina said. She sat thinking about the business manager. 'I noticed he's a smoker—at least, there was ash in the car, but I shouldn't think he'd been drinking, had he?'

'Not that I could tell,' Piers confirmed. He gave a long sigh. 'You certainly bring excitement into my life, young woman. Things are always happening when you're around.'

She gave him a dark look. 'I shall ignore that. As far as I'm concerned, all that's happened to me is my white jeans and trainers getting mussed up.' She brushed at a patch of mud on her knee.

'Yes, sorry about that. But if you will go dancing around muddy motorcars. . .' He laughed softly as she lifted despairing eyes to heaven and let out an exaggerated breath.

They had arrived back at the hospital and he drove on to the nurses' hostel. 'A pity the day had to end like this. You'll hand in our quiz entry on time, won't you?'

'Sure will, after all our efforts. Go on, you'd better check up that they're giving our patient the five-star treatment,' she said.

'Let's hope he's not been rubbing anyone up the wrong way lately in A and E,' Piers rejoined.

'Why, is he an abrasive sort of person?'

'Oh, business managers are rarely popular,' he pointed out. 'I dare say you won't be feeling too friendly towards him if he turns down your ward plan.'

She laughed. 'See what you mean. All the same, I hope the poor guy's all right. I wonder how he came to skid?'

'I'll tell you when I find out,' he said.

With a mixture of longing and regret she watched the car disappear down the driveway, wondering if she was wise to encourage this friendship. Every meeting with Piers only deepened her desire for something more. She had hoped, after today's excursion, that he might invite her to the centenary ball, but although it had been mentioned he hadn't asked her. Oh, stuff him! she thought edgily. In any case, the object of her journey to England was not to find romance, it was to get to know her mother's family. Going back to her room, Christina determined to telephone Herne Bay while she had time on her hands. Piers was right there, about her reluctance to make the next move. Yes, she was being a wimp to hold back. After all, it was easier for her to call them than the other way round. In fact, for all she knew, her aunt and uncle might already have tried and not been able to reach her. Searching out some small change, she went along to the communal payphone to make her call.

'Oh, it's you!' Aunt Beth sounded quite cheerful when she answered. 'I wondered when we should hear from you again,' she said airily.

'Well, I was waiting until I knew more about my off-duty,' Christina explained. 'Being a new girl, I'm having to fit in with the established staff, and it's a busy time at the moment, with people starting holidays. How are you? Better than you were, I hope.'

'Yes, thank you, dear. I've just fixed myself up with a new home help, although goodness knows if she's going to be any use,' Aunt Beth lamented. 'Anyway, when did you want to come? Don't make it a Saturday—your uncle usually has a wedding to cover then. And Justin often works on a Saturday too—you know what the property market's like. By the way, that girl he brought along when we had dinner the other day, she seemed a bit of a flighty piece to me. Henry says I shouldn't make spot judgements——' she gave a short laugh '—but that's me—I always say what I think.' Her aunt paused for breath, but cut in again as Christina began to speak. 'That doctor friend of yours, though, he seemed a really nice man. You'll bring him when you come, won't you? I mean, we owe him hospitality, after what he did for Justin. That boy—he should never have gone into his own flat! He brings all his washing home anyway. At least, he did. We haven't seen too much of him since we've been back. Busy chasing after that girl, I expect. . .'

Her aunt sighed deeply, giving Christina the chance

to get a word in. 'Oh, Donna's all right,' she said. 'I guess she was a bit uptight on first meeting you. Not everybody is at their best with strangers.'

'That's what Henry said. Well, he's used to it, meeting strangers and putting people at their ease, getting them to smile, that sort of thing. I expect you thought he went a bit over the top, making all that fuss of you. I thought it was silly, and I told him so. Enough to put you off.'

'No, I thought he was lovely,' Christina said warmly. 'He made me really glad I decided to come over.'

'Oh!' was all her aunt said.

They went on to talk about Christina's free time, and made a tentative dinner date for two Sundays ahead. 'I'll have a word with the others and let you know if they can all make it,' Christina promised.

'If they can't, wait until they can,' Aunt Beth promptly returned. 'I don't want to put on a special meal for nothing, if you know what I mean.'

'No, of course not.' Christina had put her last coin in the box. 'Well, my money's run out, so I'll have to say goodbye for now,' she said. 'Give my love to Uncle Henry, and I'll let you know if that's a firm date.'

With a sense of relief she put down the receiver. Well, she had done it! She had made the contact, but what to make of her reception was equivocal. Her aunt had this seeming air of grievance. It kept people at a distance and Christina wasn't at all sure of her welcome. Was she being hypersensitive? Time would tell, she thought philosophically. But how could two sisters be so totally different? She thought of her own mother—fair where Aunt Beth was dark—and with a natural dignity, charm and friendliness that had made everybody love her. Tears threatening, Christina hurried back to her room, mourning for days that were gone.

* * *

Returning to work at lunchtime on Friday, Christina learned that they had a new patient in one of their side-wards.

'Colin Rhodes, aged forty-three,' Patrick said, at the tail-end of his report. 'He came to us for a few days because ours was the only side-ward free at the time. Concussed after an RTA. Nobody could say quite how long he'd been unconscious. No apparent skull fracture. He sustained a dislocated right shoulder—reduced and immobilised in A and E. It's been dislocated before, he says, so they may consider surgery later. He's on management here—something to do with hospital finances. Let him see that the money's well-spent in our department, eh, girls?'

Patrick looked at the call-board as a patient's light flashed. 'There goes his buzzer now. Christina, you take him on. He's not a bad guy, but finding life a trial with only one usable arm.'

Without stopping to explain that she had already met the patient in question, Christina stepped along to the private room.

Clad only in maroon-coloured poplin pyjamas, Colin Rhodes sat heavily on the side of his bed. 'Nurse, would you mind helping me with my dressing-gown?' He paused, looking worried and taking short, shallow breaths. 'It's rather awkward one-handed. I'd like to go to the bathroom—mustn't embarrass any of the ladies.'

'No!' She smiled and tied his pyjama cord securely before reaching for the striped silk robe hanging beside the bed. Helping the stocky man to his feet, she fed the good arm into the sleeve, placed the gown around his shoulders and over his high-slung right arm, tying the sash neatly in front.

'Now, if you wouldn't mind helping me there—only I do detest using those bottle things,' he said.

'You haven't been to the bathroom before?' she

asked pleasantly, conscious of his laboured breathing and the look of strain. 'It's just a few steps along the corridor, but I can get a wheelchair if you're feeling wobbly.'

'I'll be all right,' he returned impatiently. 'Bit of exercise—get my circulation going—lying around's no good for anyone.'

He gave her a slight smile and she wondered if she was imagining that bluish tinge to his full lips. 'Come on, then, but take my arm.' She held the door open and saw him into the bathroom. 'Ring when you're ready,' she said. 'Don't try to manage. I'll come and get you.'

Patrick was about to go to lunch, leaving Christina in charge. 'Before you disappear,' she said, 'did Mr Rhodes have any rib damage? I haven't caught up with his notes yet.'

'There was a chest X-ray, but no fractures reported. A fair bit of bruising, though. Why?'

She shrugged. 'His breathing seems very laboured.'

The charge nurse lifted a questioning eyebrow. 'He's supposed to be for discharge tomorrow. What's on your mind?'

'I don't know. He just didn't seem too well...'

Patrick thrust out his bottom lip. 'Keep an eye on him,' he said, handing her the ward keys.

Christina went back to the bathroom and looked in. Mr Rhodes was by the washbasin, rinsing his free hand under the tap. She pulled out a paper towel from the fixture and dried his large fingers.

'Thank you. Do you do this—for all your customers?' he asked, between breaths.

She grinned at him. 'All one-armed patients get personal attention, Mr Rhodes. Not that we have many of them on this ward.'

'Have we met before?' He sounded a little puzzled.

She helped him back to his room. 'Yes, we have,

but I don't suppose you remember much about it. I was with Dr Conrad when he found you stuck in the ditch.'

He smiled carefully, his face still stiff from healing cuts and abrasions. 'Ah! Thought I recognised—that voice from somewhere. It's lucky for me that you happened to be passing.'

'What caused your skid?' she asked.

'My windscreen shattered. Must've hit a flint or something. Couldn't see a thing. I was trying to push the glass out, when my shoulder went and I lost control. 'That's the last—thing I recall—until I was—lifted on to the stretcher.' He was having difficulty with finding enough breath to go on.

'Nasty! How are you feeling now?'

'As if I've—just run a marathon. There's a stitch in my side—and I've got a headache.'

'Have you? Well, get back to bed, and then I'll see what you're written up for,' she said kindly.

Helping him off with his robe, she buttoned his pyjama jacket, noting the uneven rise and fall of his chest. Once he was in bed she checked his pulse-rate. It was worryingly fast. 'Show me, where's the pain, Colin?'

He put a hand to the left side of his chest. 'It's more a kind of tightness here—but I expect that's the bruising.'

'Probably.' She studied his medication sheet. 'I'll be back in a moment.'

Leaving the side-ward to get him some tablets, she was more than pleased to see that the registrar was now in the ward. He was on his own and talking to one of his patients. Bingo! Christina thought. When he'd finished there, she would ask him to take a look at Mr Rhodes. It would save having to send for Amy, the overworked house officer.

Donna was also on duty that afternoon, and making herself scarce while Piers was about. Finding her tidying the stock-room, Christina was reminded of the proposed dinner date at Herne Bay and she seized the chance to mention it.

'Oh, great!' Donna enthused. 'I know I've got that weekend because I'm working this one. Does Justin know?'

'I haven't spoken to him about it,' Christina said. 'Shall I leave that to you?'

'Fine! He's meeting me from work tonight. I'm sure it'll be all right, though. And I'm glad it's with you and Piers—in case Justin's mother gets one of her attacks. He says they can be frightening. I shouldn't know what on earth to do.'

Christina smiled. 'She seemed all right when I spoke to her on the phone the other day. I haven't asked Piers yet either. He's in the ward now,' she said. 'Keep an eye out for me—don't let him get away. I need him to have a look at Mr Rhodes.'

When she returned to give the pain-killers to her patient, Christina's heart sank as she came to the bedside. She had been gone barely five minutes, but now Colin Rhodes looked in real distress. He lay back against his pillows, his face cyanosed and sweaty, his breathing ragged.

'All right, Colin,' she said quietly, and, lifting the piped oxygen mask from the wall behind his bed, she positioned it over his nose and mouth. 'Take a few breaths of this and you'll soon be feeling better.' She pressed the emergency buzzer. 'Will you get Piers *now*, please?' she said urgently, when Enid's enquiring face appeared around the door. 'It may be a pneumothorax!'

In a few moments the registrar arrived, calm and controlled, enquiring what had happened.

'He just walked to the bathroom and back, complained of a headache and a pain in his side. I went to get him some pain-killers,' Christina explained, 'and

I came back to find him with a breathing problem.'

Piers took out his stethoscope and listened to Colin's chest. 'Hmm,' he said, after a thorough examination. 'You do seem to have a problem there, old chap. I think one of your lungs has sprung a leak. There's air building up in the pleural cavity, and it's the pressure which is giving you the pain. We'll get you along to the treatment-room and tap it off.' He smiled benignly at the patient. 'You lie back now and take it easy. Leave this to the experts.'

Turning to Christina, Piers went on, 'Let's do it straight away. Come on, I'll help you move the bed. . .' He released the brake with his foot and started pulling. 'Then I'll need to see his chest X-ray, if someone would like to find that for me.'

'Enid, will you?' Christina said, pushing from the other end of the bed as they transferred Mr Rhodes to the treatment-room.

'Fine,' Piers said, the procedure completed. 'Then we'll need some diazepam, and Lignocaine, as soon as I've checked this. . .' He took the X-ray, which Enid had brought to him, and slotted it into the viewing box.

Leaving Piers explaining to the patient, as only he could, how he was going to insert a chest drain to stop the lung collapsing completely, Christina hurried to get the drugs required. She recorded the prescribed dosages in the 'Controlled Drugs' book, getting Piers to sign it. She waited while he carefully checked the site for the incision which needed to be made, then held Colin's hand tightly while the doctor injected large quantities of the anaesthetising drug.

'Sorry if I hurt you, Colin,' Piers murmured. 'That's the worst part, if it's any consolation. It should start feeling numb pretty soon now.'

Waiting for the drugs to take effect, the nurses laid up a trolley with the equipment needed for the chest drain. Christina checked over the assembled items.

'Syringe, swabs and lotion, scalpel, forceps. Trocar, plastic tubing, silk sutures, the drainage bottle. And some wide elastoplast for fixation. Is that everything?' she asked the doctor.

He looked and nodded, pulling on his rubber gloves. 'We're ready to start, I think. Can you feel this, Colin?'

The diazepam having taken effect, happily the patient was pliant and submissive, scarcely aware of what was going on around him. Enid supported him while Christina draped a sterile towel around the area where Piers had decided to go in.

Patrick, back from lunch, viewed the proceedings and asked if Donna could watch. 'It'll be valuable experience for her,' he said.

Raising no objection, Piers got on with his work. 'I'm using the second intercostal space,' he said, feeling his way carefully. He made a small incision with his scalpel before introducing the long steel trocar and tubing, pushing it home into the pleural cavity.

During this operation Donna, who had been biting her lip tightly, slid to an untidy heap on the floor.

The first part of his task accomplished, Piers straightened up and glanced at his stepsister. 'Look after her, someone,' he said with a quiet smile. 'We all know the feeling.'

Christina went to her assistance. She laid the girl straight with her head on one side, then she tapped on the dividing glass wall to signal to Patrick that help was required.

Meanwhile, Piers withdrew the trocar and clamped the tubing. Back at his side, Christina connected it to the underwater drainage bottle. The clamp removed, air bubbled freely into the bottle. 'Beaut!' Christina exclaimed.

'Yes, "beaut" is the operative word.' Piers gave her a sideways smile. 'I'll suture now.' He got on with fastening the tube into place.

In due course Mr Rhodes was transferred back to his room, his breathlessness relieved. Christina anchored the drainage bottle to the side of his bed. 'Don't let anyone lift this above the bed, Mr Rhodes,' she warned. 'Would you like some tea now?'

'I certainly would.' He caught her hand, giving her a grateful smile as she prepared to leave. 'Thank you, Nurse. You've been terrific.'

'All part of the ward nine service.' Making her escape, she found Queenie in the kitchen and asked her to take in the tea.

On her way to the staffroom to see if Donna had recovered, Christina passed the doctor's office. The door stood open and Piers was there at his desk, writing industriously. She was tempted to stop and mention her aunt's invitation, but on second thoughts decided she shouldn't disturb him to talk about personal matters. Continuing on to the staffroom, there she found Donna being comforted by Enid.

'She's feeling terrible because she passed out,' Enid explained. 'I've told her it's nothing to be ashamed of. She's not the first and she won't be the last. I saw a young houseman fade away during a laparotomy once.'

Donna blew her nose. 'Piers will think I'm worse than useless,' she sniffed. 'What did he say?'

'Nothing, honestly,' Christina told her. 'He just asked for someone to take care of you. Anyway, how are you feeling now?'

'OK—just kind of stupid. What must Mr Rhodes think of me?'

'Donna, it happens,' Christina returned with a light laugh. 'And Mr Rhodes was far too dopey to remember anything. He didn't comment. Look, would you like to go home now? We can manage.'

'No, thanks all the same. I'm off at four-thirty in any case,' Donna said.

'Well, take it easy. Finish your tea—don't rush.'

Christina gave the girl a sympathetic smile. 'You could sit down quietly and write up your Kardex,' she suggested. She left to tidy up the treatment-room, packing up the instruments for return to the central sterilising department.

Piers came to find her. 'Oh, there you are.' He handed her a form. 'Patrick's not about. We need another chest X-ray for Mr Rhodes, just to make sure the tube's properly sited. They'll have to come here to do it. Can you send someone to take this down?'

She nodded. 'Will do.'

'And if Colin asks questions, this is not a long-term job. All things being equal, I'll be able to clamp the tube tomorrow and take it out the day after.' Piers bunched his stethoscope more tidily in the pocket of his white coat. 'Donna OK now?' he asked.

'Yes, she's fine. Just feeling embarrassed and in need of your—absolution, I think.'

'My *what*?' he asked with a humorous frown.

Christina smiled. 'She feels she's let the side down. A few kind words from you wouldn't go amiss, when you have the chance. By the way, Piers, I've been in touch with my aunt. We're all invited to dinner on Sunday week. Is that all right with you?'

He pulled out his pocket diary. 'That's the day after the centenary ball.'

'So it is,' she said.

'It's going to be a busy weekend.'

'Is that a yes?'

He restrained a grin. 'I wouldn't miss it. I'll be back later to check up on that X-ray.'

When he had gone it struck her forcibly that although the ball had been mentioned yet again he still hadn't personally invited her. Well, he wouldn't, would he, if he wanted to play it cool? she thought sadly. Maybe she wouldn't go to the wretched thing. Tickets were probably sold out anyway. She went to find one of the auxiliaries to take the request to X-Ray.

Visitors had begun to arrive. Among them was a woman in a smart red suit who approached Christina in the corridor, looking very concerned.

'Nurse,' she said, 'can you tell me what's happened to Mr Rhodes? I didn't like to wake him—he seems to be sleeping heavily. But what's happened? Why this contraption in his side? Someone should have let me know if things were going wrong.'

'Are you a relative?' Christina asked.

'Yes, I'm his wife, and apart from his shoulder he seemed all right when I left him last night.'

'Well, he still is all right, Mrs Rhodes. Don't be alarmed,' Christina said. 'He had a slight breathing problem—a small air leak from one of his lungs. It's not uncommon in men of his age. It might have healed spontaneously, but Dr Conrad decided it was better to relieve the pressure, as your husband was rather distressed.'

The woman tutted. 'He's such a baby—never could stand pain. Did he make a fuss?'

'No, he was quite stoical, in the circumstances.'

'Well, I want to talk to Dr Conrad, if he's about.'

'All right, I'll see if we can get hold of him. He's only recently left the ward, as a matter of fact. If you'd like to sit with your husband, he should be more awake fairly soon. I'll send you in some tea,' Christina placated.

She found Patrick, now back in the office. 'Oh, yes,' he nodded, when Christina explained about Mrs Rhodes and her demands. 'I met the lady yesterday. Piers was bound for A and E when I last saw him. If he can't make it I'll have a word with her myself.'

'Thanks, Patrick. I'll leave it with you, then.'

She was about to get on with her work when the charge nurse called her back. 'Sweetie,' he said, 'you going to this bash next Saturday?'

She paused, wondering what was coming. 'I haven't made any plans,' she said. 'Are you?'

He pulled a mournful face. 'I've got two tickets—but my girlfriend's walked out on me.'

'Oh! Sorry about that, Pat. Maybe you'll make it up before the big day.'

'No way!' he declared. 'I've just found out she's been two-timing me for weeks. We had an almighty row. It's over.' He hesitated. 'I suppose—I know this seems a bit of a cheek, but if you're not going with anyone else, would you like to come with me? No strings, but I'd as soon take you as anybody.'

Christina smiled. 'Why, thanks, Pat. I'd be delighted,' she said.

His friendly face beamed. 'Thank *you*, kiddo! You've made my day.'

'Listen, Patrick,' she said, 'seriously, if you should make it up with your girlfriend and want to call this off, no sweat. I shan't mind.'

'No fear of that,' he reassured her. 'Nobody takes me for a ride and gets away with it.'

She went on her way, her heart lighter. Funny how life could change in a flash, she thought. Doors could open in the least expected places.

CHAPTER NINE

THAT weekend the ward was far too busy for Christina to give more than a passing thought to the centenary fair. On Saturday morning they admitted Tessa Franks, a twenty-year-old shop assistant in a diabetic coma. It caused them some concern until she finally rallied after receiving a massive injection of insulin. Then, on Sunday afternoon, in the middle of visitors, elderly Mr George West, on bed-rest for his heart problem, decided to discharge himself.

Donna, on duty with Christina, came hurrying down the ward to find her. 'Mr West has pulled off his monitor leads,' she flapped. 'He's getting dressed to go home—I couldn't stop him—says he's worried about his dog. . .'

It was known that seventy-five-year-old Mr West lived alone. 'I don't remember hearing he had a dog.' Christina frowned, walking quickly with Donna back to his bedside. 'No mention of that in his case-notes.'

'Well, a neighbour promised to look after it for him—but he hasn't heard from her.'

'George,' Christina said gently, closing the bed curtains again as she slipped between them, 'you're not really well enough to go home yet, you know. Why don't you sit down in your chair and tell me what's wrong? Maybe we can do something about it.'

The old man started to cry. 'My dog—Jock—he's all I've got, Nurse. He's my best mate—I want to make sure he's going to be all right—in case anything happens to me.'

'Then we must try and make sure nothing does happen to you,' Christina said. She stooped down to take off the shoes he had been struggling to push on to his puffy feet. 'Come on, love. You need to take it easy for a little while longer. How about if I ring your neighbour and find out what's going on?'

'She's not on the phone,' he said, his bottom lip quivering. 'She's got two kids, and her husband's away, and she does a part-time job. Said she'd come and see me. She hasn't been, but I know she's got a lot on her plate. I thought she might've come this afternoon. . .'

Christina pondered for a moment. It being Sunday, she doubted whether she could get hold of the hospital social worker, but there must be something she could do to put his mind at rest. 'Look, leave it with me, George. Let's get you back to bed, and put these leads back on—then I'll make some enquiries.'

After linking him up to the monitor again and making sure that Mr West had done himself no real damage, she set off back to the office to make a few phone calls. A little while later she was able to tell him that she had contacted the police, who had promised to send someone along to his home to investigate.

'I'll let you know the minute they come back to us,' Christina promised, and within an hour she was passing on the glad news that he had no need to worry.

'Your neighbour has a cold, George,' she told him. 'That's why she hasn't been to see you. She thought it best not to spread her germs, which was very thoughtful of her. But everything's all right with your dog—they're enjoying looking after him. And the local policeman is going to keep an eye on things.'

George's tired eyes brimmed with tears again. 'Thanks, love. She's a nice young woman,' he quavered. 'I hate to give her all this trouble.'

Looking on with concern, Donna came up with an idea of her own. 'I know where there's an animal sanctuary. If you really think it's too much for your neighbour, my boyfriend and I could take the dog there for you, for the time being,' she suggested.

Reaching for a fresh tissue from the box on his locker-top, George blew his nose. 'That's very kind of you, Nurse. He'd be happier where he is, if Eileen can manage. But if it should—come to the worst. . .'

'Oh, it won't come to the worst,' Christina returned cheerfully, plumping up his pillows. 'Just you relax and get better. We'll make sure Jock's in good hands, whatever happens.' She stayed to take his blood-pressure and chatted for a moment afterwards. 'What kind of a dog is Jock?'

'A West Highland white,' George told her. 'He's ten years old now, but he's still full o' beans. Not a creaky old chap like me.'

She laughed and told him about the 'large dog' they'd had to search for on the Treasure Hunt.

Leaving Mr West to settle down, she said to Donna as they walked away, 'Luckily, that little upset didn't cause any serious damage. I'll get Amy to come and check him over, though. We don't want to risk an arrest.' Christina smiled at the younger girl. 'By the way, that was a nice thing you did, offering to take his dog to a sanctuary. Piers would like that.'

Donna's cheeks went pink. 'We-ell, I couldn't bear seeing him cry. I've got a soft spot for George—he's a sweet old thing.'

The house officer came promptly when Christina called her and explained about the patient's anxiety. 'I'm glad you were able to sort it out for him,' Amy said. 'He still needs complete bed-rest for a time. We'll have a case conference and see what help we can get him when he does go home.'

Afternoon tea was being taken round to the patients by the time Amy had finished having a friendly talk with Mr West. She returned to the office, and a few minutes later Christina took tea to the busy young doctor, who was sitting writing up her findings.

'Ooh, thanks,' Amy said gratefully. She laid down her pen to take a sip. 'I must have a look at that diabetic girl while I'm here. What's her blood sugar doing now?'

'It's coming down. It was fifteen at midday. She's OK, but none too co-operative. She's loath to accept she's got a problem.'

Amy shrugged sympathetically. 'Faced with a lifetime of blood-monitoring and diet restrictions, that's not uncommon. I'll get the diabetic liaison nurse to come and counsel her.' Turning to a more cheerful subject, the HO went on, 'I managed to find time to buy a new dress for the ball next Saturday, since Himself actually did me the honour of inviting me. And what do you bet there'll be some kind of emergency and I shan't get to wear it? That's what happened at my last place.'

'I'll keep everything crossed for you,' Christina said, smiling, although she felt a stab of envy. So that was who Piers was taking! Well, no doubt Amy knew all about his hang-up on the romance front. And maybe he felt it safer to spread his favours around. Thanks to Patrick, however, Christina would not be without a partner. And with any luck she might even get to dance with the bedevilling registrar—the man she was trying so hard not to love.

After the weekend, news of the success of the fair began trickling through. Ward nine's knock-out team had won the event, much to everyone's jubilation. Full details of other prize-winners and the monies raised on stalls and side-shows were to be announced at the ball.

On Tuesday morning Colin Rhodes had his chest drain removed, having suffered no set-back after it had been clamped the previous day. In the treatment-room Christina produced suture materials for Piers to close the incision. That done, he ordered removal of the stitches in a week's time.

'You can come back to Outpatients for that, so you could go home this afternoon, or whenever it suits you.' Stripping off his rubber gloves, Piers added jokily, 'I'm quite sure you can't wait to see the back of us.'

'On the contrary, I've enjoyed the experience, in a masochistic sort of way.' Colin shot a flirtatious grin in Christina's direction.

She smiled back and picked up his pyjama jacket to help him into it. 'Nice of you to say so.'

'And shall I get this free in time for the ball?' he asked Piers, indicating his strapped shoulder.

'That's up to the bone boys, but I should think so. If you do, I shouldn't advise getting too physical too soon, knowing your history,' Piers said.

'Then I shall come and claim you for a dance, Christina,' Colin declared as she tied the sash of his dressing-gown. 'You'll be there, will you?'

'Yes, I'll be there.' Conscious that Piers was turning a frown in her direction, she added flippantly, 'Shall I hold you to that?'

'My pleasure—if I make it. Actually, my stay here has been quite an eye-opener,' the business manager went on. 'Nothing like being a patient to find out what goes on at grass-roots level.'

Piers coughed politely behind his hand. 'May I point out that you've been in a rather privileged position, Colin?' His eyes glinted mischievously. 'And may I also point out that Christina, here, was the originator of that ward plan I showed you, shortly before you were laid up? Did she mention it?'

'Oh! So it was you!' The business manager turned a mock-solemn face to Christina, shook his head and tutted. 'Do we have a dissident here, Doctor?'

'I prefer to call it initiative,' Piers rejoined. 'She'll

be telling you next that her mother trained here and wouldn't be pleased with the status quo.'

'In fact she'd be astounded at the blatant introduction of unisex,' Christina put in.

Colin Rhodes laughed softly. 'We must all move with the times, my love.'

The registrar's expression gave nothing away, but Christina sensed that this man was not one of his favourite people. 'If I don't see you before you leave, Colin, take care,' he said smoothly, and left the treatment-room.

'Are you going to telephone your wife,' Christina asked, concentrating on clearing up her trolley, 'or would you like me to do it for you?'

'No point. I know she's out this morning. She'll be coming this afternoon in any case.' He paused before going back to his room. 'But thanks for the offer. And don't think I haven't appreciated your many kindnesses,' he murmured, squeezing her shoulder.

Piers had apparently found it necessary to return to the treatment-room. Poking his head in, he said briskly, 'Tessa Franks' file, Christina—will you find it for me, please, and bring it to my office?'

She raised her eyebrows, but nodded. 'Excuse me,' she said to the business manager, and went along to do as she'd been asked. Finding Sister Helen seated at her desk in the office, Christina explained, 'Piers is chasing Tessa Franks' file.' She flipped through the notes trolley. 'It's here all right. Why couldn't he have got it himself—or asked you?'

Helen stopped poring over the off-duty roster she was sorting out. 'Your guess is as good as mine,' she said. 'I'm through with trying to understand doctors. All I know is they usually prefer to be waited on. . .'

Christina extracted the file and took it along to the doctor's office. 'It wasn't missing,' she made a point of saying. 'It was where it ought to be.'

'Ah, thank you.' Piers took the folder, but called her back as she turned to leave. 'Who's taking you to the ball, then?' he demanded.

'Patrick,' she said.

He scratched his cheek, eyeing her thoughtfully. 'I didn't know you and he were dating.'

'We're not—*dating*, as such,' she emphasised. 'He just asked me to go with him on Saturday—that's all.'

Piers played with his fountain-pen, running it between his long fingers. 'If you hadn't made plans I would have asked you myself.'

'Amy told me you were taking her,' she replied.

'So I am—and a number of other guests. That way it cuts down on the gossip. You were to be included.'

'Was I? Well, you didn't say, and I'm not a thought-reader. I'll save you a dance, if you can tear yourself away from your other guests,' she said airily. 'Anything else?'

The bewitching hazel eyes narrowed. 'Why are you sounding aggrieved?'

'I'm not,' she returned. 'Neither am I your personal handmaiden.'

'Oh, dear! You are in a mood. Well, before that glare freezes my guts—is it still on for dinner at your aunt's on Sunday?'

'Well, yes, but——' Christina hesitated '—don't feel obliged, if you've changed your mind. I can make your excuses.'

'No, I haven't changed my mind. Just checking—in case you'd prefer to take Patrick,' he quipped.

A reluctant smiled curved her lips. 'Thanks, but my aunt's invitation was for you, and I wouldn't dare change partners.'

'Fine. Now, shall we both get back to work?'

He turned his attention to the file she had brought, and she walked away, uncertain who had won that particular skirmish.

Later that afternoon, meeting Donna in the staff-room as they both prepared to go off duty, Christina said chattily, 'Are you bringing Justin to the ball on Saturday?'

'Actually no, we're not going.' Donna's cheeks flushed. 'I'm taking him to Broadstairs—to meet my mother and John—that's Piers' father.' She drew a long breath before going on. 'Please keep this under your hat, but Justin and I have decided to get married.'

For a moment Christina was dumbstruck. 'You have?' She struggled to keep the dismay out of her voice. 'That's a bit sudden, isn't it? I admit you do seem to have hit it off amazingly, but—you've hardly had time to get to know each other, have you?'

'I expect that's what everyone will say—but it's long enough.' There was an anxious edge to Donna's smile. 'We don't need more time—we just know it's right for us.'

Karen, walking in at that moment, interrupted the confidences. 'Hi!' she said, going to her locker. 'What are you two plotting?'

Christina laughed. 'Nothing important—just wondering what to wear for the ball on Saturday,' she fabricated.

'Oh, that,' Karen shrugged. 'Not going, myself. Not keen on dancing.' She collected her holdall and shoulder-bag. Going to the mirror, she pulled a comb through her straight brown bob, examined a pimple on her chin, said, 'Cheerio!' and walked out.

Donna blew air between her pursed lips. 'Phew! Thanks. I don't think she heard anything. Anyway, as I was saying, about Justin and me—— Look, have you got time for a coffee downstairs? I simply must talk to someone about things.'

'Sure!' Questions were spilling over in Christina's head. Even if Donna's mother proved agreeable, Christina felt certain that there would be objections from Justin's side of the family. And she also had a hunch that blame for this whirlwind romance could easily land up on her own doorstep somehow.

Once they were seated in a quiet corner of the canteen, the bubbly young student nurse began to unburden herself. 'I know you probably think we're crazy,' Donna said, 'but there's no point in waiting when you're absolutely sure, is there? And Justin's got a secure job—there are no financial problems.'

'But what about your career, Donna?' Christina queried. 'Will you carry on with your training?'

'We-ell, for the time being. . .'

'It would be a pity to have got so far and then give up. You never know, you might be glad to be properly qualified one day.'

Donna didn't answer. Christina went on, 'Have you told Piers?'

'Good heavens, no! He's bound to disapprove.'

'And has Justin said anything to his folks?'

'Not yet—we plan to tell them on Sunday, when the right moment comes.'

It was Christina's turn to say, 'Phew!' She looked into the other girl's eager young face. 'Well, I do wish you both all the luck in the world. It may be a bumpy ride,' she warned.

'We both know that, and we don't care, so long as we've got each other,' Donna said.

Christina had been looking forward to the weekend, especially the chance to meet with Piers in a proper social setting, but now Donna's secret weighed heavily on her mind and she viewed the prospect with certain misgivings. Attempting to rationalise, she told herself firmly that it was not her problem. It would therefore be stupid to spoil Patrick's evening on Saturday by letting it worry her. Sunday would have to take care of itself.

The ball was being held at the Connaught Country

Club, set in attractive parkland some two miles from the hospital. Patrick had been there before and told Christina it was very up-market. She decided against buying anything new for the occasion, however, and settled on wearing a favourite filmy black dress. No one over here had seen it before, in any case.

On the festive evening Patrick duly arrived, by taxi, to collect her. In dinner-jacket and black bow-tie, his wiry sandy hair brushed into place, he looked neater than she had ever seen him. 'Mustn't risk being done for drink-driving, and I mean to enjoy myself tonight,' he said. Letting out a low whistle, he stood back to admire her attractive appearance, creamy shoulders framed in the silk chiffon, a single strand of pearls around her throat. It being a warm evening, there was no real need for the exotic silk shawl draped over her arm.

'Hey! You look terrific, baby!' Patrick exclaimed. 'You're ten times prettier than that bitch who ditched me,' he declared, helping her into the cab.

She laughed softly. 'So absence hasn't made your heart grow fonder?'

'No way! Plenty more pebbles on the beach. But I certainly picked a winner for tonight.' He squeezed her hand, and Christina had the impression that he might already have started celebrating.

When they arrived in the grand foyer of the country club there were already people clustering around a blackboard which stood alongside the table plan. It showed the results of all the centenary events, and the current financial picture.

Pushing forward, Patrick craned his neck to see the outcome of the special inter-ward competitions. 'In first place, A and E ties with ward nine,' he read. 'Oh! Well, we should get half a prize. Better than nothing, eh?' A proprietorial arm around her, he kissed her cheek.

She had not been aware that Piers was anywhere near, but his seductive voice beside her made her turn and look up.

'So, our efforts weren't entirely in vain,' he remarked lightly.

'No,' she returned, her manner pleasant but detached. 'I don't suppose this will get us a new ward layout, though.'

He pursed his lips. 'Maybe not. You'll have to continue working your charms on Colin Rhodes.'

'Is he here?' she asked.

'Yes—I saw him in the cloakroom.'

Patrick had been checking their table number. 'Oh, that's nice,' he breezed. 'We're all together. I wonder who fixed that?'

Christina went along to the cloakroom to leave her shawl. In the pink and white ladies' room she found some of the others who were on Piers' table. There was Amy, and Bridget from Radiology, and Gloria—the senior sister on ward ten, Women's Medical—plus their partners. And there was Judy, who had come with Will.

'Hi!' Judy said, radiant in cherry-red satin. 'I hoped you'd be here. Who did you come with?'

'Patrick. I'm helping him mend a broken heart,' Christina explained.

'Oh! I wondered if Piers might have asked you,' Judy murmured.

'No—I don't think Piers intends to be linked with anyone in particular,' Christina observed with a slight smile. 'Come on, shall we go?'

They went out to join their menfolk.

The MC announced, in resounding tones, that dinner was about to be served, and people began making their way to the glittering ballroom. It was laid out with flower-decked round tables for ten, and one long top table for the hospital heirarchy and VIPs.

Christina found herself seated between Patrick and Piers—a situation not altogether to her liking. With Piers in such close proximity it wasn't easy to remember that her partner for the evening was Patrick. Fortunately, Patrick himself seemed unaware of any such problem. He always had a flow of small talk, and with wine loosening his tongue as the evening progressed he radiated *bonhomie*.

Even so, with Piers commanding much of her attention, Christina could never quite forget Donna's little time-bomb which would await them at their dinner date tomorrow.

She started almost guiltily when, glancing around between courses, the registrar remarked casually, 'I don't see my stepsister anywhere...'

'No, she told me she was taking Justin home to Broadstairs.' The minute Christina had told him that she wished she hadn't.

Piers frowned. 'Oh? Not like Donna to miss out on a party. I haven't forgotten a birthday, have I?'

She shrugged. 'How would I know? You must ask her yourself tomorrow.'

The meal ploughed its way through to the coffee and liqueurs, after which came the inevitable speeches, the toasts, and the votes of thanks.

'Terrific!' exclaimed Patrick, finishing his cognac at the end of the proceedings. 'Now we can get on with the best part—the dancing. I'll show you how to get rid of your inhibitions, Chrissie.'

Christina giggled. 'I'm hanging on to mine, Patrick. You can do what you like with yours.'

Dance music was well under way by the time she and Judy returned from freshening up in the powder-room a few minutes later. The live band had started with a rousing, vibrant number. Grabbed by Patrick as soon as she reappeared, Christina entered whole-heartedly into the spirited session, at the end of which they both flopped, breathless but exhilarated, on to their chairs.

'That was terrific, kid. You're a great mover.' Patrick eased a finger inside his collar and mopped his brow with a handkerchief. 'Would you like a drink?'

'Yes, please. A long one—an iced lemonade would be nice.' Idly watching his spasmodic progress to get it, as he frequently stopped to chat to other friends, Christina turned to Judy and smiled. 'I wondered if it might be uphill work with Patrick tonight, but he seems as wacky as ever.'

'Mmm,' Judy agreed. 'Nice guy, Patrick. Do you fancy him?'

'Not especially. I'd never even thought about him in that light,' Christina admitted. 'I do like him—but. . .'

'He doesn't light your fire,' Judy finished for her, laughing. 'Oh, well, all dates don't have to end in bed.'

The music began again, a slow blues number, and Christina found Piers standing in front of her holding out his hands. 'Shall we?' he invited.

Her heart pumping wildly, she rose and went into his arms.

'Patrick certainly knows how to unwind,' Piers said, guiding her effortlessly to the romantic strains of a nostalgic number.

'Yes, that's his main purpose tonight. To put the past behind him.' She explained about the recent collapse of his love life.

'Oh! Tough luck. Well, the remedy seems to be working.' His steadfast eyes meeting hers, Piers' expression was quizzical. 'Don't fall for catching him on the rebound, will you?' he warned. 'In any case, I wouldn't have thought he was your type.'

Her body, moulding to his, was too close for sanity, too dangerously pliant. She felt he must sense her pulses throbbing. 'And what is my type?' she asked levelly, endeavouring to put space between them.

'I don't know. I'm trying to find out.' His smile was tantalising, his arm around her deliciously exciting. 'You know how I like to get to the bottom of things,' he said, giving her a slight squeeze.

'No need to worry about me,' she returned. 'Patrick and I understand each other. If I can help him over a bad patch, that's what friends are for, isn't it?'

'A noble sentiment—but don't be so naïve,' he scoffed. 'The guy obviously fancies you—and it's all too easy to give the wrong impression. As I very well know.'

'Oh! So because of one bad experience you're determined to stand on the sidelines for the rest of your life, are you?' she challenged.

'Is that how you see me?'

'Yes, when I bother to think about you at all,' she fibbed.

For a moment he was silent, his concentrated gaze causing a commotion inside her. 'You look very lovely tonight,' he said suddenly. 'I like your dress.'

The compliment took her by surprise. She flashed him an impudent grin. 'Thank you. I must be very careful not to read anything into that!'

Pulling in his chin, he gazed at her under frowning brows, before saying softly, 'You should have been spanked when you were knee-high, my girl.'

'Oh, stop being Victorian. And that was my toe you just trod on.'

'Sorry. I can't measure up to the wonderful Patrick as a mover, especially when you're being argumentative. Allow me to concentrate, will you?'

'Perhaps you'd like me to count?' she mocked.

'Belt up, woman!' Then both his arms were around her, folding her to him. Involuntarily her own arms slid about his neck; she couldn't seem to help herself. The strobe lights danced about them and the singer with the band crooned something about not being in love. . .

They finished the rest of the dance not speaking. But Christina knew his lips were on her hair as he hummed along to the music. There was an undeniable alchemy between them, a certain chemistry that made her feel that this was where she belonged. It was impossible to think he did not share her elation as they moved around the dance-floor in close harmony.

'There's your drink,' Patrick said, pushing it towards her when they returned to their table. 'I got held up. Anything for you, Piers?' He waved his hand over a selection of cans on the table.

'Thanks, but no. I ought to circulate.' The registrar excused himself and went away.

Throughout the rest of the evening partners were interchanged. Everyone declared it a fantastic night, but although Christina was never without a partner she felt wretched that Piers didn't come to ask her again. On one occasion when he sat out she caught him scowling in her direction as she bopped merrily with Patrick. Perversely, she redoubled her efforts to concentrate on her partner. If Piers disapproved, too bad!

In due course Colin Rhodes came to claim his promised dance with her.

'You're a popular lady,' he said. 'I wondered if I was ever going to get a look-in.'

She laughed. 'Good to see you here, Colin. Does that mean you're feeling OK now?'

'Yes, fine. I thought I ought to put in an appearance—after all the efforts people have been making. It's been a splendid drive all round. And now we shall have the unenviable task of apportioning the profits.'

'Mmm—I suppose that won't be easy,' she agreed, thinking of her ward plan but deciding it best not to mention it. 'What happened about your car?' she went on. 'Was that beyond repair?'

'I believe so. The garage said the chassis was ruined. Still, these things happen. And I'm counting my blessings that it wasn't my own chassis which was a write-off.'

Christina's laughter bubbled out. 'Yes, you were very lucky.' At the end of the dance she felt happy with the way that encounter had gone. After all, if she'd made a favourable impression with Colin, that might well tip some cash ward nine's way.

Patrick had been growing more affectionate by the minute as the evening wore on, his arm around her at every opportunity. Flattering though this was, she found his advances embarrassing, especially as she couldn't bring herself to reciprocate. It was a relief when he disappeared occasionally to the cloakroom, or someone else claimed his attention.

Towards the end of the evening, during Patrick's absence, Piers came and sat beside her. 'Do you want to dance with me again—or do you have more respect for your toes?' he asked.

'I'll risk it—if you'll promise not to lecture me,' she said.

'I don't make promises I can't keep.' He swung her on to the dance-floor, imprisoning her body against his. 'You seem to have been enjoying yourself hugely tonight,' he remarked.

'Yes, I really have. Haven't you?'

'Let me ask the questions. So where does it go from here, with Patrick, after this?'

'Back to as we were, I dare say. Tonight was just a bit of fun, to help lift his spirits.'

'That's not the impression I get. Patrick seems well and truly enamoured, if you ask me.'

'Well, I didn't. And don't glower—it doesn't suit you.'

'Then don't make me.'

Christina gave an indignant laugh. 'So it's my fault you're in a foul mood?'

'Yes—you've spent most of the evening flirting outrageously with Patrick.'

Her eyes widened. 'I take exception to that. Anyway, what are you really trying to say—that you actually mind?'

'I certainly wouldn't give it my blessing.'

'Oh, dear! That bad?' She put on a penitent face.

He dug his fingers into her ticklish rib and she couldn't restrain a giggle.

'Christina!' Piers sighed. 'What am I going to do about you?'

Acting on impulse, she reached up to brush his tempting lips with hers. He raised his eyebrows. 'Come on, is that the best you can do?' His mouth took possession of hers, and if he hadn't been holding her so firmly she felt that her legs might have folded. The intensity of his kiss left her breathless, wanting more. Oh, God! she thought wildly. What have I started?

'OK?' he murmured presently, his cheek against hers.

She nodded, not trusting herself to speak. His nearness was erotic, mind-blowing. There were no further demonstrations of affection, but she knew there could never be anything between herself and someone like Patrick, when one lingering kiss from Piers could fell her defences.

At the end of the music balloons were released from the ceiling and there was a mad, laughing scramble to catch and burst them. Piers secured one for her. She carried it triumphantly back to their place, only to have it popped by Will.

Then came the last dance and a final bopping session. Most people resumed their original partners, so that for Christina there was no escaping Patrick's now amorous attentions. She accepted his advances with good grace, but found herself unable to respond.

'Your heart's not in this, is it?' Patrick said, his pleasant face questioning.

'No, not really. I'm sorry, Patrick,' she murmured abjectly.

He hugged her. 'Don't worry about it, Chrissie. I kind of sussed there was competition.'

'Patrick, you're a lovely guy,' she said. 'I'm sure there'll be some lucky girl along for you soon. But it's not me.'

Later, as Christina waited in the crowded foyer while Patrick checked on their taxi home, Piers sought her out. 'So I'll collect you at five tomorrow?'

'Yes, great. Thanks, Piers. What would I do without you?' she joked.

'Tell me about it some time!' he retorted. 'Are you going to be all right, going home with Patrick?'

'Of course I am. He's not stoned, is he? Only slightly happy.'

'Huh! There would have been room for you in my mini-bus. See you tomorrow, then.' He went away to find Amy and the rest of his party.

With his arm companionably around her in the taxi, Patrick said, 'Coming back to my place for coffee?'

'Better not,' she said. 'That would mean calling out another cab to take me home.'

'You could always stay the night. . .'

She laughed. 'It's not on, Patrick. No toothbrush, and nothing to change into tomorrow. It's been a great party, but I'm really knackered.'

'Yeah, me too,' he said, yawning. 'Some other time, maybe?'

'Maybe. Thanks for asking.'

Two a.m. found her ready for bed, trooping along to the kitchen in the nurses' hostel to make herself a hot drink. There she discovered Judy, still in her finery, filling the kettle.

'Hi!' Christina said. 'Weren't you meant to be going back to Will's place?'

'That was the general idea,' Judy moaned, 'but he got called in for an RTA practically as soon as he put his key in the front door. So it was goodnight, Judy. How about you? All quiet on the Patrick front?'

Christina smiled. 'Yes, that's what I intended, and he wasn't unduly bothered, thank goodness.'

They made their drinks and took them back to Judy's room, where they stayed talking until Christina could no longer keep her eyes open. Once she was in bed, however, sleep was elusive, with thoughts of Piers running riot in her head. Was he actually at last beginning to break out of his protective shell? And was he really beginning to show interest in her as a person? She could only hope that events tomorrow would not ruin what had started to seem vaguely promising.

CHAPTER TEN

THE light shafting through the folk-weave curtains at her windows awoke Christina on Sunday morning. She lay for a time collecting her thoughts. They were obsessed with Piers. Had he guessed how deeply in love with him she was? Try as she might, it was practically impossible to disguise her feelings when his very nearness made her body ache for him.

But how did Piers feel about her? He had pointedly shown disapproval when other men paid her attention, and his returning kiss—after her own impulsive gesture—had been passionate and forceful. Even so, she was far from convinced that he was ready to commit himself where love was concerned.

Now, trailing along to the bathroom, Christina paused to look out at the bright morning, her thoughts still with the dynamic registrar, trying to figure out how he would react to Donna and Justin's news. Whatever he personally thought, she guessed he would be a calming influence in what might well be a difficult situation. Christina could only regret being unavoidably linked with the romance. However, there were still a good few hours to pass before that had to be faced, and before she would be meeting the spellbinding registrar.

She sighed, wishing they had met in different circumstances. But if Piers had made up his mind to live like a monk, then she was determined not to go to pieces over it. The solution was to get on with living—move away if necessary.

At five o'clock that afternoon Christina waited downstairs for her escort. Wearing a lilac figure-fitting summer frock, sunglasses sitting across her gleaming blonde hair, she breathed deeply, making an effort to quell her rising excitement at the prospect of spending time with the man she craved. In her shoulder-bag was an opal pendant which she had brought as a gift from Sydney for her aunt. Maybe that would help create a favourable atmosphere, she hoped.

Piers drew up in the BMW, seductively attractive in stylish casual trousers and navy blazer over a cream sports shirt. He greeted her with that quiet half-smile that was guaranteed to make her blood surge.

'Hello!' he said, his thrilling voice compounding the effect of the smile. 'You got home all right, then?'

'Yes, thanks. No problem.' She took her seat beside him, tossing her white jacket into the back of the car, and they set off straight away.

'So Patrick behaved himself?' Piers continued.

'Impeccably. But then I've always had the impression he's a decent sort of guy.'

'That's as maybe. I shouldn't make a habit of being his shoulder to cry on, though.'

'I don't intend to,' she said.

Piers suddenly pulled into the parking bay opposite a small row of shops. 'I ought to take your aunt a present. She could be allergic to flowers—chocolates be all right?'

'Fine, I should think. Actually I do have a present for her myself,' Christina told him. 'An opal pendant which I brought from home.'

He smiled. 'Then she'll feel thoroughly spoiled. Won't be a minute.'

She watched him stride purposefully into the small newsagent-confectionery shop and reappear with a sizeable box in a paper bag. Throwing it on to the back seat, he remarked wryly, 'I've a feeling we may need all the sweeteners we can use today.'

'Oh? Why's that?' Christina asked levelly, although her stomach knotted.

'My father rang me this morning. He says Justin and Donna have announced their intention to get married—as soon as possible.' Piers shot her a discerning glance. 'You don't look surprised—did you know?'

She nodded, feeling guilty and catching her bottom lip between her teeth. 'Donna did mention it to me.'

'Why didn't you say something yesterday?'

'She asked me not to, so I couldn't, could I? Anyway, it's their news—it's up to them when they want it broadcast.'

He gave a short laugh as he started up the car again. 'Yes, I suppose you're right—but I'm glad I've been forewarned.'

Christina groaned. 'I almost wish I hadn't been. It's awful to be sitting on a secret and wondering when it's going to pop out. It's like knowing the worst and being powerless to stop it happening.'

'Now you're being melodramatic,' Piers accused. 'All you need do is be your calm, together self and we'll see what happens. Donna's usually adept at getting her own way. Let's hope your aunt isn't too disturbed by the speed of events.'

Christina was feeling anything but calm and together. 'How did your father and Donna's mother take it?' she asked.

'Dad was fairly non-committal. I think he was hoping I could persuade them to wait. Donna mentioned a register office ceremony in a month's time. But I don't have any influence with her. Even if I wanted to interfere, it's hardly my place, is it?'

'She's very much in love,' Christina returned quietly.

Watching the countryside flash by, she was reminded of that time, some weeks before, when they had seen Justin and Donna disappear into the empty house. All too soon they were driving up the same tree-lined avenue, but today Justin's car was not in evidence when Piers drew up in the road outside.

'We seem to be first,' he said. 'Good; that will give you a chance to talk to your folks before my stepsister takes over.'

As they walked up the drive together, Uncle Henry opened the front door, a smile of welcome on his rugged face. 'Hello!' he boomed, coming to meet them and kissing Christina warmly. 'Wonderful to see you again. And you too, sir,' he added, gripping Piers' outstretched hand. 'I hope you're taking good care of this lass for me. She's the daughter I never had, you know.'

With his arm around her, he ushered them into the house, calling, 'Beth! Christina's here.'

Her aunt came hurriedly down the blue-carpeted stairs. She was dressed in a smart floral two-piece, her dark hair short and stylishly blow-dried.

'Henry! Must you make so much noise?' she said with a strained smile. 'Shut the front door, please. Hello, Christina!' After pecking her niece on the cheek, she gave Piers a coy smile of welcome. 'Dr Conrad—I'm so glad you could come.'

'Piers, please.' With a charming smile he handed her the chocolates. 'Sorry these aren't gift-wrapped.'

She peeked inside the paper bag. 'Oh, thank you so much! How lovely—can't remember when Henry last bought me chocolates. He's so busy taking photos of beautiful brides, he forgets he's got a wife.'

Christina produced her gift. 'Well, here's a little memento of Australia for you, Aunty. Hope you like it.'

'Dear me! I am being made a fuss of,' her aunt laughed. 'What's this?' She stripped off the wrapping-paper and opened the small, velvet-lined box. Inside lay a richly iridescent opal in a filigree gold setting, on a fine gold chain.

Having taken some trouble choosing it, Christina watched her aunt's face eagerly.

'Oh, very nice, dear,' Beth said, 'but aren't opals supposed to be unlucky, unless it's your birthstone? I'm a Virgo—that's a sapphire.'

Looking over her shoulder at the jewel, Henry said, 'Surely you don't believe all that stuff, Beth? I think that's gorgeous—a sweet thought, Christina.'

Beth snapped the case shut. 'Yes, thank you, dear,' she said matter-of-factly. 'I hope Justin and his young lady won't be too long. He's not the best of timekeepers. Henry, why don't you serve our guests some drinks on the patio? I've got a few bits and pieces to see to in the kitchen.' She flitted away.

Henry led them through to where cushioned garden furniture was tastefully arranged on the paved area outside. After pouring their drinks, he placed his arm around Christina's shoulders and murmured, 'Don't mind Beth's manner, my love. She was pleased with your gift, but she gets embarrassed easily. She's never been good with words.'

'That's OK.' Christina was determined not to let her aunt's attitude bother her, although she had been disappointed at the time.

'What a wonderful garden,' Piers put in, gazing down the length of the colourful vista. It was bright with roses and a multitude of other flowers, set off by a sizeable velvet green lawn. 'Is gardening a hobby of yours, Mr Wells?'

'Not especially. We have a man to do the hard work,' Henry admitted. 'My hobby, as well as my work, is photography. I must get some shots of you both before you leave.' He gave a sigh of pleasure, his eyes focused on Christina. 'I just can't get over how like your mother you are.'

'Uncle Henry,' Christina ventured, setting down her dry Martini, 'what exactly was the trouble between

Mum and Beth? My mother never told me.'

Seeming vaguely uncomfortable, Henry glanced towards the house, making sure his wife was not within earshot, then he cleared his throat. 'The simple truth is Beth was jealous of her sister. Elfrida was bright, she was beautiful—and Beth thought I was in love with her. Well, in a way I was, but not in that way, although we were both fond of each other. Anyway, the girls had an almighty row about it, and that was when Beth's asthma started. I won't go into more detail, but it was—well, that sort of thing. . .'

'Oh!' Christina said flatly.

Piers sipped his drink. 'Family squabbles can start over the silliest misunderstandings,' he remarked lightly.

Other voices signalled the arrival of the remaining two guests and in the next minute Justin and Donna appeared on the patio.

'Hi!' Justin exclaimed, coming to greet them. 'My two life-savers! Great to see you both. Hi, Dad!'

There were kisses and handshakes and a general feeling of camaraderie. Donna was quieter than usual, and she looked a litle pale. Having been let into the secret, Christina wondered how long it would be before it was burst upon their unsuspecting hosts.

'Come along, everyone, the meal's ready,' Beth called from the patio doorway.

In the cool dining-room the polished mahogany table was tastefully set with rose-pink place-mats, polished silver and crystal glasses, rose-pink paper napkins folded into water-lily shapes.

'Oh, isn't this pretty?' Donna picked up one of the folded napkins. 'You are clever, Mrs Wells.'

'I try,' Beth simpered. 'Sit down, all of you. I hope everyone likes avocado with prawns. Justin, pour the wine, darling.'

There followed a succulent meal of roast loin of pork

with all the right trimmings, finishing with a light fresh fruit Pavlova. Whatever her faults, Christina's aunt Beth merited full praise for her cooking.

'That,' announced Piers, laying down his spoon and fork together, 'was the finest meal I've had in a long time. Here's to the cook!' And he raised his glass to her.

'Yes,' Christina agreed, 'that was great.' Smiling towards her aunt, she also raised her glass.

'Er—while we're drinking toasts,' Justin said, looking a little bashful, 'Donna and I have something to celebrate. We want to tell you that we've decided to get married.'

There was a startled silence. Henry was the first to recover his breath. 'Well, congratulations, son. I can't say I'm surprised. Donna's a very lovely girl.'

Beth also recovered her powers of speech. 'Married?' she rapped out. 'Do you mean—engaged?'

Justin laughed. 'That too, only we haven't had time to buy the ring yet. And yes, I do mean married, in four weeks' time.'

His mother's jaw gaped. 'B-but you can't mean it,' she spluttered. 'Wh-why the rush?' Her wide-eyed gaze fell on Donna. 'Are you pregnant?' she demanded.

On the point of tears, Donna shook her head vigorously. 'W-we hoped you'd be pleased.'

'Mother! How could you?' Justin flared.

'Well, you can see what everyone will think,' she retorted grimly.

Henry jumped up and came around the table to kiss Donna. 'My dear, we're delighted to welcome you into the family, although I must admit it is something of a shock. You are perfectly sure about this?' Turning to Piers, he added, 'What do you think?'

Piers spread his hands. 'It's their future. I can only wish them well if this is what they want. After all, they wouldn't be the first couple to make a snap decision, having found each other.'

'Huh! Has everyone lost their senses around here?' Beth flashed.

Christina had been gazing from one to the other, her mouth dry. She felt she should say something, but couldn't find the words. Her aunt's suggestion of pregnancy had shaken her, and one or two things stirred uneasily at the back of her mind—like Donna's queasy stomach when they had been on early turn together. In spite of the girl's denial, Christina wondered if her aunt had hit on the truth. She swallowed, and went around the table to kiss her cousin and Donna. 'Congratulations, both of you,' she said warmly. 'I think you're perfect for each other.'

'Huh!' her aunt repeated, glaring at Christina. 'If it hadn't been for *you* they'd never have met.'

'That's true,' Justin laughed. 'Many thanks, dear cousin.'

Christina began to clear the table and Donna joined her. 'Oh, God! Wasn't that ghastly?' she whispered in the kitchen.

'Never mind, it's over now,' Christina returned.

'If only it were! I've a feeling it's only just beginning,' Donna sighed.

Shortly after they'd had coffee, Piers said it was time they were going. 'I need to call in at the hospital,' he explained, 'and I'm sure you've got a lot to talk about here.'

Not much more of any significance had actually been said on the proposed marriage, but the air was crackling with unspoken thoughts. Christina was glad to be leaving. Extra voices in a family argument could only confuse the issue, and her aunt actually seemed more annoyed than distressed.

'I feel a bit mean, abandoning Donna.' Christina chewed her thumbnail as she and Piers drove away.

'There's no reason why you should. It's not your problem. And sometimes the only way to learn is the hard way,' he replied.

Studying the determined set of his jaw, she said, 'Don't you have the weeniest bit of sympathy for them? Aunt Beth can't be the easiest person to deal with.'

He turned her a sideways smile when they halted at traffic-lights. 'Perhaps you can see now why your mother fell out with her. Much as you love your relatives, it's not always possible to get along with them.'

'Mmm,' she agreed. 'Their problem was not such a dark secret after all.' She paused. 'Why do you have to dash back to the hospital?'

'I lied,' he admitted cheerfully. 'I thought you looked worried—and I could think of better things to do than getting involved in someone else's problem. How about coming back to my place for some more coffee?'

Her heart lifted joyfully. 'That sounds better,' she agreed.

They made the journey quickly through the darkening countryside, presently bypassing the floodlit tower of the great cathedral. Soon afterwards Piers turned the BMW in through the wooded drive of the luxury flats, parking conveniently in a lay-by opposite the security doors.

His ground-floor flat was in the same state of happy disorder that she remembered from last time—journals piled high, bits of the Sunday newspaper strewn over the coffee-table, reference books and a scattering of ballpoint pens on his desk.

'Make yourself at home,' he said, stripping off his blazer, collecting an empty lager can from the desk and making for the kitchen.

She draped her own jacket over a chair, picked up a used mug from in front of the sofa and followed him into the kitchen. 'Anything I can do?' she asked.

'I am capable of making coffee on my own,'

he smiled, 'but stay and entertain me.'

She perched on a stool at his breakfast-bar and sighed. 'I'm out of lightweight small talk. My head's too full of the Herne Bay dramatics. Thank goodness Beth didn't throw a wobbly—but you heard what she said about if it hadn't been for me Justin and Donna wouldn't have met.'

Piers poured boiling water on to the ground coffee in the cafetière. 'If it hadn't been Donna, your aunt would have lost Justin to some other girl sooner or later. Or maybe it was fated to be this way.'

'Oh, don't talk about fate,' Christina despaired. 'You heard what she said about that wretched opal being unlucky...'

'If she thought it, she shouldn't have said it. That was very uncalled for.' Piers reached for two mugs from the cupboard. 'Pass me that tray, will you?'

She passed him the melamine tray, and he assembled everything necessary and carried it through to the living-room, putting it on the low coffee-table.

'I guessed I should end up getting the blame,' Christina continued mournfully. She took a seat on the sofa and kicked off her white sandals.

Piers sat down beside her and pressed a finger on her nose. 'I repeat, not your problem, and nothing you can do about it. So put it out of your mind and relax.' He poured the coffee. 'Tell me about your long-term plans.'

'Haven't got any. When I first came here I suppose I was hoping to find myself a ready-made family—but I don't think I fit in at Herne Bay. Now I'm not sure what I shall do.'

'Dear me! Is this the dynamic young nurse I've been getting to know and admire?' he teased.

She smiled wryly. 'I feel far from dynamic. More like crawling into a bolt-hole and staying there.'

'A little moral support needed, I think.' He stretched

out an arm behind her shoulders. 'Come and have a cuddle.'

'And I don't know if that's a good idea either,' she returned.

'Well, how will you know unless you try? Come on, you can always slap my face if I should get carried away,' he joshed.

'In the remote possibility that you did, don't think I wouldn't,' she declared.

But the ambience was too potent to be resisted. It was ecstatic to be invited to snuggle into the crook of his shoulder, to lay her head against his broad chest, to feel the strong beat of his heart through the thin fabric that divided them. She wished she could stay there forever.

Stroking her hair, Piers murmured huskily, 'And why should you think it a remote possibility that I could lose my head over you?'

'Because you're not given to losing your head, are you?'

'No, not often. But I am human, therefore far from perfect, and at times out of my depth. Do these buttons undo?' He ran his fingers down the front of her dress.

'No, they're just decorative.' A *frisson* ran down her spine.

The telephone shrilled, breaking into her rising tension. She eased herself from his arms as the phone continued to ring.

'Hadn't you better answer that, Piers?'

'Hell! I must get a phone with a better sense of timing.' He kissed her lips briefly but fiercely before leaping for the offending instrument on his desk. 'Yes?' he barked.

Listening to the one-sided conversation, Christina gathered that the caller was Amy and that there was a patient in Casualty about whom she was concerned.

'Adrenalin wasn't effective—and you've given

aminophylline IV?' Piers queried. 'What's her name? Pulse-rate 120? All right, I'll come. Meanwhile, try her with hydrocortisone 200mgs, stat.'

Putting down the receiver, Piers looked at Christina, his expression guarded. 'That was about your aunt,' he said. 'She's been brought in by ambulance—suspected status asthmaticus. We have to go.'

Christina caught her breath. 'Oh, no!' she murmured, wriggling into her shoes and smoothing her hair. 'She must have got into a state soon after we left. I thought her reaction was too good to be true.'

They hurried out to the waiting car and within ten minutes were arriving at the hospital.

'I'd better come in with you,' Christina said. 'I expect Uncle Henry will be needing support.'

'Yes, you do that.' Piers was already striding into the busy department. One of the casualty officers met him and took him to where Aunt Beth was being looked after in the resuscitation-room.

Seeking a familiar face among the night nurses, Christina spotted Yvonne on her way to the reception desk. 'Mrs Beth Wells—asthmatic—she's my aunt,' she explained. 'How is she?'

'Your aunt?' Yvonne paused in surprise. 'Not responding too well to the drugs so far, I'm afraid. The medical reg has just arrived to see her.'

'Are her husband and son here?' Christina asked.

'Yes—they're in the relatives' room,' Yvonne told her. 'That second-year Donna Bryce is with them, too. She's very upset.'

'OK; thanks. I'll find them.' Christina hastened to the comfortable room set aside for the use of distressed relatives. She tapped on the door and looked in. Justin and Donna were there, sitting side by side. Her uncle Henry sat on his own, head bent, hands hanging limply between his knees. All three looked up anxiously when she entered.

'Hello,' she said gently. 'Piers has just been called in to see Aunt Beth. What happened?'

Donna started to cry. 'Don't, darling,' Justin murmured, putting his arm around her.

Henry blew his nose. 'She had one or her attacks soon after you left. She was letting rip about what the neighbours would think if Justin didn't have a proper wedding—and what was she going to tell her friends at the Women's Institute? But Justin insisted nothing would change their minds.' Henry cast a baleful glance towards his son. 'She began to sound wheezy and had difficulty getting her breath. I got her the spinhaler and Ventolin. They usually do the trick, but this time they didn't. She began to panic and started gasping, saying she was going to die.'

Donna tearfully went on with the story. 'I tried to reassure her that the feeling would pass, but she was fighting for every breath and going blue in the face—so Mr Wells called their GP.'

'He came pretty quickly and gave her some adrenalin—like he did when she got uptight about me getting my own flat,' Justin went on. 'Only this time it wasn't effective, so Dr Allen called for an ambulance. What's going on now—do you know?' he asked worriedly.

'I imagine she'll be getting some oxygen in Resus,' Christina told them. 'Piers will make sure she gets everything she needs. Try not to worry,' she said. 'It takes time for the drugs to have effect.'

Although wanting to be reassuring, she was well aware that even with the best of care a happy outcome could not always be guaranteed.

'It was terrible to see her fighting for breath and knowing it was all our fault,' Donna said tremulously.

'We offered to put off the wedding—we couldn't do more than that,' Justin flared.

'You might have been a bit more considerate in the first place,' Henry growled. 'You shouldn't have sprung it on us like that. You know your mother and how emotional she is.'

'Honestly, Dad, you know it would have been the same whenever we'd told you,' Justin argued.

'I'm ever so sorry,' Donna said miserably.

'Well, she's in good hands now,' Christina offered peaceably. 'Let's hope she'll soon be back to normal.'

The door opened again and the duty sister came in. 'Mr Wells,' she said kindly, 'your wife is not responding as quickly as we would like. Dr Conrad is getting her a bed in Intensive Care, just in case she needs more help with her breathing. You can come and see her for a few minutes, while we make the necessary arrangements.' She looked around the room. 'Just you for the time being, sir. She couldn't cope with a lot of visitors.'

Henry followed her from the room.

When he had gone Christina tried hard to be supportive to the young couple, who were obviously feeling the burden of guilt. 'It's so easy to be wise after the event,' she said.

'Yeah,' Justin sighed. 'Whatever I say, I usually manage to get it wrong.'

Donna had been sitting with her arms folded across her stomach. She looked pale and wretched. 'Excuse me,' she suddenly said, 'I must go to the loo.'

Christina looked at her, an intuitive feeling making her worried. 'You OK?' she asked. 'Shall I come with you?'

'I'll be all right,' Donna said, making for the door.

'What's wrong?' Justin demanded.

'Emotional upsets affect people in all sorts of ways,' Christina returned. 'I'll go and see how she is, just in case she's feeling faint. Justin. . .' Christina hesitated '. . .could Donna be pregnant? You can tell me—I won't talk.'

Her cousin looked sheepish, and nodded. 'That's

why we wanted to get a move on. No question of her wanting to get rid of it—she was thrilled to bits.'

'I'd better see if she's all right.' Christina hurried along to the toilets. 'Donna?' she called softly. 'Are you there? Everything OK?'

A muted response came from behind the closed door and in due course Donna reappeared.

'It's happening!' she said, her face tragic. 'If I thought we needed to get married pretty damn quickly, we don't now. I know I've lost it. My inside's been churning for hours. Oh, bloody hell!' She burst into stormy tears.

Christina put her arms around the girl. 'Oh, Donna! Never mind,' she murmured soothingly. 'Maybe it's for the best, the way things are.'

They waited a little while, giving Donna time to compose herself before going back to Justin, by which time Henry had also come back to the rest-room.

'They say it may be necessary to put her on a ventilator, depending on how she responds to the drugs in the next few hours.' Henry mopped his brow with a crumpled handkerchief. 'God! What a day.'

Piers came in, his presence heartening. 'I think we're winning,' he told them, 'and you really can't do any good by staying here. She just needs peace and rest. Why don't you all go home and get some sleep? We'll call you should it be necessary.'

It was decided that Henry would go back to sleep at Justin's flat, to be within easier reach of the hospital. Christina said goodbye to the three of them at the door of Casualty and went back to find Piers before going home herself. She caught him about to leave the doctor's office.

'Oh, Christina,' he said, 'your aunt's already gone to ITU, I'm afraid. Were you hoping to see her?'

She shook her head. 'I'd be like a red flag to a bull. I expect she blames me for the whole shambles.

No, I just wondered how she really is.'

'I'll walk you to your room and we can talk on the way.' Piers led her in the direction of the exit.

Soon they were out in the cool, night-scented air, with the stars making a bright canopy overhead. And now he put his arm around her waist and drew her close. 'Say your prayers tonight,' he said. 'Your aunt should rally—and she is in the right place should urgent measures be needed—but I hope they won't be.'

'Thank you, Piers. You're a great comfort,' she said.

'A comfort? You make me sound like a hot-water bottle.'

She smiled. 'You know what I mean.'

'I don't know that I do. But, depending upon the course of events, perhaps you'll give me the opportunity to find out one day.' Outside the nurses' hostel he ran his hands down the satin coolness of her bare arms. 'What happened to your jacket?'

'Oh! I must have left it at your place.'

'Well, at least that gives me the excuse to ask you to come back for it,' he murmured. 'Goodnight—and don't lie awake all night worrying about your aunt, will you? That's an order.' He placed a light kiss on her forehead, after which he caught her in a tight embrace, and ended by savouring her mouth in a manner which had her head spinning.

Upstairs in her room Christina did a lot of hard thinking. Tonight everyone's reactions had been influenced by heightened emotions, she decided. Even the level-headed Piers. In his flat he had been tantalisingly loving towards her, and until the interruption he had seemed to be on the brink of relaxing his iron self-discipline. But there could have been a certain amount of pity in that. Piers was a compassionate man and probably felt sorry for the way her aunt had treated her. In less emotive moments, though, would he too blame Christina that her irresponsible cousin and Donna had ever got together?

She sighed heavily. How could love ever flower between Piers and herself when this problem family of hers was giving such bad vibes? His attitude towards her was bound to get prejudiced. It would have been far better if she had never got to know him, then at least she would have been spared this tearing heartache. Maybe it would be better if she went back to Sydney.

CHAPTER ELEVEN

THERE had been no urgent summons to her aunt's bedside during the night. Neither was there any reply from Justin's flat when Christina phoned at eight-thirty the following morning. Now, although not on duty until midday, she dressed in her staff nurse's uniform and made her way over to the hospital.

She had awoken very early after what she hoped was a nightmare but which daylight confirmed to be only too true. The dinner at her aunt's last night had been a disaster, and the beginnings of her intriguing interlude with Piers had been cut short by her aunt's collapse. So much for my efforts at goodwill! she despaired.

As she approached Intensive Care her anxiety increased; she wondered what lay ahead. Had Henry and Justin been called during the night? And would her presence be welcomed? If the very worst had happened it would be her fault for setting all these events in motion.

There was no one at the nurses' station when Christina arrived. She waited uncertainly until a nurse in a blue trouser suit emerged from one of the rooms.

'Hi!' the girl said cheerfully. 'Can I help you?'

'Please. I believe you've got my aunt here—Mrs Beth Wells. How is she?'

'She's your aunt?' The girl's eyes strayed to Christina's name-badge, showing her status. 'She's OK. We didn't need to ventilate after all. We're keeping her on metered oxygen for now, but I guess she'll soon be transferred to a medical ward if she continues to improve.'

Christina put her hands together in relief. 'Oh, thank God for that.'

The other girl smiled understandingly and pointed to a door. 'She's in there. You can go and see her in a minute, when the doctors come out.'

'I don't want to risk upsetting her again.' Christina looked vaguely apprehensive. 'I was part of the family row that triggered this attack.'

'Oh, I'm sure it'll be all right,' the nurse said. 'She's quite peaceful now. See what the doctors think.'

As she spoke Piers and Will, in their white coats, both came from the room in question.

Will held out an arm towards her. 'Oz! You have no right to look so absolutely beautiful at this hour of the morning!'

The ITU nurse grinned and went on her way.

Christina half smiled and looked from Will to Piers. 'Beth is all right, then?'

Will glanced from one to the other. 'Yes, you can fill her in on things, can't you, Piers? I have to get on.' And he left them.

Her heart hammering, Christina felt the need to break the silence as her eyes met Piers' steady gaze. 'From Will's manner do I take it the crisis is over?'

'That crisis, yes,' the registrar said, straight-faced.

'Why—is there likely to be another?' Christina asked, frowning.

'Not with your aunt, I trust.' Piers hesitated. 'You haven't heard about Donna?'

A shiver slid over Christina's skin. 'What about Donna?'

'She was brought in early this morning. Query ectopic.'

Christina stared at him in dismay. 'Oh, my God!' she murmured, her mind going back. 'Late last night she told me she was having some spotting. I should have made her see someone then.'

'So, you knew she might be pregnant?' he asked.

'Well, not until then. She hasn't ruptured, has she?' Christina asked anxiously.

'I haven't spoken to the gynae reg yet. I understand she'll be going to Theatre shortly.' The registrar paused. 'Don't mention this when you see your aunt, will you? She shouldn't be worried.'

'No, of course I won't.'

'And there's nothing anyone could have done about it. It happens,' Piers said by way of comfort.

'Does her mother know yet?' Christina asked.

'Yes, my father is driving her over. Sorry I can't stop to talk—I've got an outpatient clinic waiting.'

As she watched him go, Christina's throat ached with unshed tears. That's life, she thought sadly. Sometimes you had to take what it dished out. This must have screwed up her chances with Piers completely, but it was a tragedy for Donna, who had wanted her baby.

Taking a deep breath, she squared her shoulders and put on a pleasant face as she entered the four-bedded ward. Her aunt was propped high on pillows, the oxygen catheter in her nostril taped into place. She lay with her eyes closed, but was breathing regularly.

'Aunt Beth?' Christina said in a gentle voice, taking her aunt's hand.

Beth opened her eyes. 'Oh, it's you,' she sighed.

Christina smiled. 'Feeling a bit better now?'

'Yes,' her aunt returned feebly. 'I nearly died, you know.'

Christina made a sympathetic face. 'It was a rotten thing to happen, after your lovely party, too. Never mind, you'll soon be up and about again.'

'No thanks to you!' Beth's manner was hostile. 'Why don't you go back where you came from?' she snapped. 'You brought us nothing but trouble.'

It was like a bucket of cold water thrown in her face. Tears very near, Christina bit her trembling lip. 'I'm sorry you feel like that. All I wanted to do was mend bridges,' she said. 'Look, I won't stay now, if it upsets you, but if there's anything I can do just let me know.' She bent to kiss her aunt's pale cheek. 'Get well soon.'

In the corridor outside Christina found Henry and Justin talking to one of the nurses. They both greeted her with muted pleasure.

'Are you on this ward?' Henry wanted to know.

'No—I just came to see Beth. She seems fairly OK now. Justin, be careful not to upset her, won't you? Keep off the subject of Donna if you can.'

He groaned. 'Oh, God! We half promised Mum we'd put off the wedding, but that's the last thing we really want to do.'

Christina felt surprised. From her cousin's response she assumed that he didn't yet know of Donna's plight, but she was too uptight herself to talk about it. He would find out soon enough. She looked at her pendant watch. 'Time I was on my way. I'm glad Beth's improving, Uncle Henry. See you again soon.' She kissed them both goodbye.

Hurrying to a nearby cloakroom, Christina let her tears overflow. What a mess everything was! And it had all begun with her stepping on a plane in the first place. The rest had followed as surely as if it were pre-ordained. She blew her nose and mopped up her face before going down to Casualty to see what was happening about Piers' stepsister.

Christina found her friend Judy on duty there. 'Hey!' Judy said. 'You look awful. What's up?'

'Piers just told me about Donna,' Christina said. 'I feel so guilty—I was with her when she had a bleed. And I did nothing. Well, I thought maybe she'd just miscalculated, or was late starting or something. And I was more concerned about my aunt at the time. Is Donna still here?'

'No—she went to Theatre about ten minutes ago.

And whatever you did or didn't do wouldn't have changed a thing, so you don't have to feel guilty,' Judy said understandingly. 'Go and put your face back on and I'll meet you for lunch at twelve, OK?'

Christina smiled wanly. 'Thanks.' She paused. 'Has my cousin been told about this yet?'

'No—there was no reply from his telephone. But her mum is on the way.'

'Well, you'll find Justin in ITU. He's there, visiting his mother.'

Later that day, concluding her report to the second-shift nurses, Helen told them, 'Tessa Franks will be going home this afternoon. Her insulin's been ordered from the dispensary but she needs a letter for her GP.' Closing the Kardex file, the sister pushed back her brown fringe. 'Some of you may have heard that Donna was rushed in for emergency surgery this morning. So we're one short today, but I expect we'll cope.'

Karen Hill rolled her eyes and muttered, 'She's useless anyway.'

The sister cast her a reproving glance. 'Come on, now, that's not very charitable.'

'What's the matter with her?' Karen asked.

'Couldn't say,' Helen retorted. 'And now's not the time to discuss it. I've been told some members of the management committee may be doing a tour of the wards this afternoon, so will everyone please make sure that everything's neat and tidy?'

Christina's head was busy with her own thoughts, but not too busy to bless Helen for her tact. In the absence of the junior she herself did a quick round of the ward, gathering up stray urinals and disposing of rubbish before starting on the two p.m. drugs.

With Enid she straightened beds and turned a couple of helpless patients, making them more comfortable. She then went in search of the discharge papers for the young diabetic, whose mother had arrived to collect her. Contacted via her bleeper, Amy promised to deliver the necessary letter for the GP as soon as she could prise it out of Piers.

'Sorry to keep you hanging about,' Christina apologised to Tessa. 'Your medication is here—we're just waiting for your doctor's letter.' She smiled at the girl. 'You will attend the diabetic clinic, won't you? And keep an eye on your blood sugar. If it's properly controlled your condition shouldn't stop you doing anything you want to do.'

'Yeah, I know that's what they say, but it's not that simple in practice,' Tessa said.

Christina went off to her own tea and, buying a chocolate biscuit, she felt a pang of sympathy for Tessa, facing a lifetime of strict diet. Returning to the ward, she found that the management team had been and gone in her absence.

'Panic over,' Helen announced. 'Colin was with them. He asked where you were, Christina. You seem to have a fan there.'

Christina responded with a faint smile. She was on her own in the office with the sister, and Helen looked at her keenly. 'What's wrong with you?' she asked. 'Anything I can do?'

'I was thinking about Donna as a matter of fact,' Christina confessed. 'Have you heard how she is?'

'Yes, she's back in the gynae ward and making a normal recovery. Nothing sinister, so they say, but that's all I know. Are you friends, then?'

'I do know her fairly well—she happens to be going out with my cousin,' Christina explained.

The day marched on busily until nine-thirty, when she was free at last to hand her ward duties over. Before leaving the hospital she checked that her aunt was still making progress, and that Donna was as well as could be expected. She had seen no more of her uncle Henry, or Justin, or Piers. Judy had come off duty earlier and had gone out. Christina felt totally isolated. Back in the nurses' hostel she armed herself with a supply of loose change and rang Justin's flat.

'Hi there!' he said, sounding fairly normal. 'Dad and I have just been out for a meal, having done our duty visiting the sick. How's yourself?'

'I'm fine. And your mother?'

'Oh, she's great. They're keeping her overnight in Intensive Care, but she'll be moved in the morning, all being well.'

'And what about Donna?' Christina asked. 'Have you been able to see her?'

'Yes, just for a few minutes.' Justin paused. 'That was tough. I suppose you heard what it was?'

'Only what they thought it might be. I haven't seen anyone to talk to since her operation.'

Justin sighed. 'I saw the surgeon—he said she was lucky not to have ruptured the tube or something. By the way, we decided to tell my mother it was appendicitis, so as not to upset her again. At least she'll be pleased we'll now have to put off the wedding for a time. I don't think Donna's mum was any too pleased with me,' he continued, 'but it takes two, doesn't it?'

Christina agreed. 'Look after her, won't you?' she said.

'Of course I will. By the way, are you still interested in finding a flat? I know of one which might suit you, near the hospital.'

'I think I'll stay where I am for the present,' Christina said, 'until I know what I'm doing.'

'Moving in with the dashing Dr Conrad?' Justin speculated.

'After all this hassle? I bet he thinks our family is the last word in stupidity,' she scoffed. 'Love to Uncle Henry—I hope he'll have Beth home soon.'

* * *

For the next few days Christina seemed to exist in a kind of no man's land. To her great relief her aunt was transferred to the adjacent women's medical ward before being allowed home at the end of the week. It could have been awkward if she'd been bedded in ward nine.

Donna's stay while recovering from major surgery was, of necessity, longer. But, visiting her, Christina found her moderately cheerful and surrounded by flowers.

'Justin's been a pet,' she chatted, 'and so has his father. I'm terribly sad about the baby, of course. But I'm going to take more care, until we're married. That first time—well, it took us both by surprise—we just couldn't help ourselves.'

Christina listened patiently, smiling, imagining the relief of Donna's family that she had decided to be more circumspect.

She was about to leave when Piers strolled to the bedside. Against the call of her heart Christina had been deliberately avoiding the registrar whenever he came to ward nine. Now she felt the hot blood flood her cheeks.

'Hello, stranger!' His direct gaze added to her confusion. 'Where have you been hiding for the last few days?' he demanded. 'I was thinking of sending out a search party.'

'Well, you know where I live, if you'd wanted to see me,' she retorted.

'Have you come to visit me, Piers, or to quarrel with Christina?' Donna asked petulantly.

'I'll be back to see you in a minute.' He walked with Christina to the door and in the corridor caught her arm. 'Have you been avoiding me?'

'Why should I?' she retaliated. 'As I said, you could've found me if you'd wanted to.'

'Oh, come on, Christina. I've been really pushed

this week. But five minutes on the ward now and then would have been appreciated. When's your next free evening?'

'Tomorrow,' she said.

'Right, you're spending it with me, so don't plan anything else.'

'Do I have any choice?'

He held back a smile. 'Certainly not. In any case, there's an item of lost property at my flat you have to collect.'

'You mean my jacket? Well, if that's all this is about, why don't you bring it in for me?'

He dug his hands into his trouser pockets. 'You know damn well it isn't. I'll pick you up at seven—and if I should be late, don't run away.'

Piers went back to see his stepsister, leaving Christina knowing that her good resolutions were about to be up-ended. Was she crazy to let herself be dictated to by this man when every step she took his way deepened her urgent need of him? Suddenly she didn't care. Whatever did or didn't happen, no other man could cause stars to burst in her head just by laying his hand on her arm.

The next twenty-four hours seemed like forever as Christina waited for her date with Piers. Hurrying off duty at four-thirty, she showered, washed her hair, painted her fingernails and toenails, and couldn't decide what to wear. It had been a chilly day and now rain threatened. She supposed they would eat somewhere but had no idea what he'd planned. Deciding not to dress up, she settled on a pair of hip-hugging white trousers and a colourful silk overshirt.

Piers was there waiting in the car, drumming his fingers on the steering-wheel, when she went down to meet him at five minutes past seven. He checked his wristwatch. 'You're late,' he said.

'Well, you said you might be, so I thought I'd wait

upstairs instead of out here. What are we going to do?'

'There's a decent pub not too far from my flat. We can eat there later, if that's all right with you?'

'Yes—great. I shall have worked up an appetite by then. Meanwhile. . .?'

'Back to my place. I need to put a razor over my chin—and you have to collect your jacket.'

They smiled at each other but said no more. On reaching his flat, he said, 'How about you making some coffee while I take a shower?'

'All right; I'll have a go at finding my way around your kitchen.'

Piers disappeared to the bathroom while Christina opened cupboards, filled the kettle, found mugs and did everything the way she remembered him doing on that awful Sunday when everything had gone wrong.

She was settled on his sofa when he came from the bathroom fastening his shirt buttons.

'This scene has a feeling of *déjà vu*,' he smiled, sitting down beside her.

She made a woeful face. 'Up to this point it was fairly OK. Scrub everything after you got that phone call from Amy.'

Piers chuckled. 'Yes, let's rewrite the script. I warned Amy, no call tonight, on pain of death.'

'You're a hard taskmaster. Shall I pour?'

'Yes, please.' He stroked back a gleaming strand of her hair that fell forward while she poured. 'If I remember rightly, last time you were here we were about to discuss those long-term plans of yours that you said you hadn't got.'

'Well, I have now. Events this week helped me make up my mind.'

He turned to face her. 'Oh? Tell me.'

'Piers, I came to find myself a family,' Christina reminded him. 'Well, I found them, but it hasn't worked out.' She blew on her coffee and put the mug down again. 'My aunt made it very clear the other day that I'd been nothing but trouble since the day I came.' Her bottom lip trembled. 'So I'm going back to Oz.'

Piers sat forward in astonishment. 'You're *what*? Just because some neurotic woman can't let go of her son?' He took her hand in his. 'Come on, Christina, I know she's given you a hard time, but you're not seriously going away because of that, are you?'

She shrugged. 'There's nothing to keep me here.'

'Isn't there?' he asked quietly. He paused for a moment while his eyes held hers. 'Look, darling girl, you may not have found a family, but you've certainly found love. I know this may sound sudden, but it's true. *My* love, and every bit of me, is yours, if you'll have me, Christina. Will you?'

She stared at him, open-mouthed in amazement. 'Piers—did I hear right? Do you mean that?'

'With all my heart, beloved. Never a day passes when I don't find myself thinking of you, wanting you, desperate if I don't catch just a glimpse of you. Please, *please* don't leave me—don't go back to Australia.' He slid down on one knee in front of her. 'Marry me—and I'll take you there for a honeymoon.'

'Oh, Piers!' She was half laughing, half crying. 'That's something I thought I'd never hear you say, after what you told me when we first met.'

'A man can change his mind. Well, will you?' he asked huskily.

She took his adorable face in her hands and placed a long, sweet kiss on his lips. 'Of course I will,' she murmured tenderly.

'Then come down here and let me show you how much I love you.'

She slid to the floor beside him and melted against the exciting strength of his powerful body. They lay together in an ecstasy of longing.

'No need to ask if these buttons undo,' he said

presently, finding his way inside her shirt and covering her softness with kisses. 'This is where your home is, dear heart. Here with me.'

Outside it had begun to rain, a thin, persistent English drizzle. Inside, their love had burst like sunbeams through a cloud.

'Will you miss the sunshine and the exotica?' he asked, his mouth against hers, their limbs entwining.

'I'll settle for this, and you, any time, darling,' she told him rapturously.

'Now you're making sense,' he declared.

It was some while before he took his mouth from hers again. 'Oh, I knew there was something else I had to tell you,' he said. 'Ward nine will be closing down for refurbishment at the end of August. They're going to put your blueprint into practice.'

'Oh, Piers, that's terrific,' she squealed.

He laughed softly at her delight. 'And the perfect opportunity for our honeymoon, don't you think?'

'And what will Aunt Beth think about that?' Christina wondered. '*Two* hasty marriages in the family? Well, I do know she likes you. It might just make her feel better about Justin and Donna's getting a move on.'

'We'll put it down to a family trait, not hanging about once you know what you want,' Piers murmured between dropping ardent kisses over her face, her throat, her shoulders.

'Do you mind?' she laughed. 'This undue haste isn't down to me.'

'Oh, yes, it is. Who was it threatened to walk out on me? Stop arguing. Just love me, darling.'

And that was a suggestion Christina had no difficulty in complying with.

"All it takes is one letter to trigger a romance"

Sealed with a Kiss—don't miss this exciting new mini-series every month.

All the stories involve a relationship which develops as a result of a letter being written—we know you'll love these new heart-warming romances.

And to make them easier to identify, all the covers in this series are a passionate pink!

Available now   **Price: £1.99**

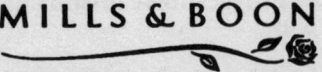

MILLS & BOON

Available from W.H. Smith, John Menzies, Volume One, Forbuoys, Martins, Woolworths, Tesco, Asda, Safeway and other paperback stockists.

Temptation

Lost Loves

'Right Man...Wrong time'

All women are haunted by a lost love—a disastrous first romance, a brief affair, a marriage that failed.

A second chance with him...could change everything.

Lost Loves, a powerful, sizzling mini-series from Temptation continues in May 1995 with...

**What Might Have Been
by Glenda Sanders**

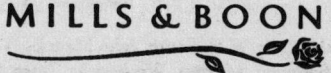

MILLS & BOON

LOVE ON CALL

The books for enjoyment this month are:

PRACTICE MAKES MARRIAGE	Marion Lennox
LOVING REMEDY	Joanna Neil
CRISIS POINT	Grace Read
A SUBTLE MAGIC	Meredith Webber

Treats in store!

Watch next month for the following absorbing stories:

TAKEN FOR GRANTED	Caroline Anderson
HELL ON WHEELS	Josie Metcalfe
LAURA'S NURSE	Elisabeth Scott
VET IN DEMAND	Carol Wood

Available from W.H. Smith, John Menzies, Volume One, Forbuoys, Martins, Tesco, Asda, Safeway and other paperback stockists.

Readers in South Africa - write to:
IBS, Private Bag X3010, Randburg 2125.

TASTY FOOD COMPETITION!

How would you like a years supply of Temptation books ABSOLUTELY FREE? Well, you can win them! All you have to do is complete the word puzzle below and send it in to us by 31st October 1995. The first 5 correct entries picked out of the bag after that date will win a years supply of Temptation books (*four books every month - worth over £90*). What could be easier?

```
H O L L A N D A I S E R
E Y E G G O W H A O H A
R S E E C L A I R U C T
B T K K A E T S I F I A
E E T I S M A L C F U T
U R C M T L H E E L Q O
G S I U T F O N O E D U
N H L S O T O N E F M I
I S R S O M A C W A A L
R I A E E T I R J A E L
E F G L L P T O T V R E
M O U S S E E O D O C P
```

CLAM	HOLLANDAISE	OYSTERS	SPICE
COD	JAM	PRAWN	STEAK
CREAM	LEEK	QUICHE	TART
ECLAIR	LEMON	RATATOUILLE	
EGG	MELON	RICE	
FISH	MERINGUE	RISOTTO	
GARLIC	MOUSSE	SALT	
HERB	MUSSELS	SOUFFLE	

PLEASE TURN OVER FOR DETAILS ON HOW TO ENTER ➡

HOW TO ENTER

All the words listed overleaf, below the word puzzle, are hidden in the grid. You can find them by reading the letters forward, backwards, up or down, or diagonally. When you find a word, circle it or put a line through it, the remaining letters (which you can read from left to right, from the top of the puzzle through to the bottom) will ask a romantic question.

After you have filled in all the words, don't forget to fill in your name and address in the space provided and pop this page in an envelope (you don't need a stamp) and post it today. Hurry – competition ends 31st October 1995.

Temptation Tasty Food Competition,
FREEPOST,
P.O. Box 344,
Croydon,
Surrey. CR9 9EL

Hidden Question _____

_____

Are you a Reader Service Subscriber?   Yes ☐   No ☐

Ms/Mrs/Miss/Mr _____

Address _____

_____

_____ Postcode _____

One application per household.

You may be mailed with other offers from other reputable companies as a result of this application. Please tick box if you would prefer not to receive such offers. ☐

COMP395